DOME EIGHT

DOME

8

TYLER BEATY

First published in the United States of America in August 2022
by See It Bee It Publishing ™
316 Redbud Ct
Sand Springs, OK 74063

Library of Congress Cataloging-in-Publication Data
available upon request

ISBN: 979-8-9868597-0-5 (pbk)

ISBN: 979-8-9868597-1-2 (e-book)

Cover illustration by Sarah Beaty
Printed by Blurb, 600 California St, CA 94108 USA

I would like to dedicate this book to my family, of course, but also to the many people that have inspired me along the way.

DOME 8

Chapter 1

Elroy awoke, bleary-eyed, and thumped his head against the roof as he tried to sit up. He rubbed his bruising forehead as he climbed the ladder down the bunk bed; the bottom bunk was empty; that was where his father slept or used to sleep, he pushed the thought aside. He entered the living room of their small apartment. The bedroom, the cramped lavatory, and the living room and kitchen. He moved to the stove, where he made some scrambled eggs and used more than his daily ration when preparing his coffee. He sat at the small table, wishing he wasn't eating alone. He swiftly changed into his work overalls and exited the apartment.

He had dirty blond hair, cloudy eyes, was a little shorter than average, and had been old enough to enter the workforce just last year, and he loved this city. He stared up at the large glass dome covering the otherwise typical city. Sure he wasn't born here, but he was only an infant when the evacuations began. He had grown up in this city. He didn't remember what fresh air tasted like; all he knew was the smog-filled air of Dome Eight.

He jogged the rest of his way, he was almost late, and when he opened the door to the squat structure that took up the majority of the block it was on," Late again, as usual," Tobias said with a smile. "It's the first time I've been late this month!" Elroy said, also smiling. He and Tobias strapped on their tool belts laden with wrenches, hammers, and screwdrivers. Tobias chuckled. "It's nice to see you. What'd you do over the weekend?" He asked. "You know me, nothing much. I tried playing some baseball, but it went pretty bad," Elroy said. Their boss interrupted by shouting, "Elroy!" And Elroy hurried into his boss's office to get his assignment for the day.

"What did you get?" Elroy said to Tobias as they prepared to leave the building. Tobias was taller than Elroy by a good few inches and had black hair waiting for an excuse to gray, despite being around the same age as Elroy. "Just some lamppost maintenance and refueling, boring. How about you?" Tobias said, "Says I'm supposed to repair one of the digging machines," Elroy said. "Digging machines?" Tobias said, clueless as ever; Elroy sighed. "The tunnel collapse that severed the telegraph and pneumatic lines?" Tobias nodded. "Well, they've decided to finally do something about it and are beginning to clear the miles of rubble," Elroy said, "I don't think it'll work. They're going to excavate what must be at least a hundred miles of rubble, going only a few miles a day? Doubt it," Tobias said. "Well, they'd better. The rations are getting worse and worse," Elroy said. Tobias shrugged. "Somebody will figure something out," He said. "And if nobody does?" Elroy asked. Tobias shrugged again, not wanting to think about it. Finally, after a few long moments of silence, "Well, anyway, the machines were built before the Flood, damn near twenty years ago. Honestly, I'm surprised they're only now breaking down," Elroy said. Tobias nodded in agreement. "That's nearly as old as the dome," Tobias said. "And we both know how leaky that thing is," He continued. After some more small talk, Elroy grabbed his duffel bag and waved goodbye as Tobias went to fix lamps.

Elroy knew the city inside and out. It was part of his job as a maintenance worker. Things broke all over the place. And as such, it didn't take him long to reach the elevator. It was big, noisy, and few people used it, but it was the only way to the lower levels, where he needed to go. "Hey," he said as he approached the elevator operator. The man leaned against the wall and stood straight to talk. "What'cha want?" The operator said, pushing up his flat cap. "I need to get down to level four," Elroy said. "Going all the way down, huh? What for?" He asked as he stepped into the elevator. "I'm going to fix some stuff," Elroy said. "That's vague," the operator said as he stepped onto the big, industrial elevator. Elroy joined him, but they had to wait until more people loaded themselves onto the elevator. Most of the people were coal miners. They were essential to the survival of the dome. However, since they were cut off from the rest of the domes, they lacked the raw materials and fuel for their large industrial machines. As an alternative, this elevator was built, accessing several levels of mines. Though they were the people supplying the dome with fuel, the stuff that kept the lights on and the air fresh, they were paid remarkably little, and the mortality rate was something that made his stomach churn. As he surveyed the group of miners, he saw several his age or younger. And he was glad he wasn't one of them. As the elevator began to descend, it made a racket. It was the sound of the motors and something metal scraping against rock. The coal miners exited the elevator on levels two and three. Elroy stepped off the elevator and out into level four.

Immediately he was greeted by the sight of two small electric carts, each carrying a crate on a bed behind the driver. As Elroy stepped off the elevator, the two carts took his place. Then, after the operator checked that nobody else was coming, the elevator rose into the darkness.

Chapter 2

He expected it to be much more claustrophobic than it was. The ceiling was three times his height, and the walls were far-reaching. This was obviously the staging area. Workers sat around chatting, and machines sat dormant. He followed the path that the many carts going to and from the elevator had made. Soon he found the end of the man-made cavern and found a building set into the stone. The building seemed to be some kind of gatehouse, as a red and white barrier stopped him from continuing down the path. Finally, somebody stuck their head out of a window in the small building. "You need to get past?" the guard said. "Yes," Elroy said. "What's your business here?" The guard asked. "I'm here to fix some run-down equipment," Elroy said. "Okay, can I see some ID?" The guard asked. Elroy rummaged around his pockets, withdrew his wallet, and handed his citizen ID card to the guard. After a few seconds, the guard handed back his card, and a buzzer sounded, and the gate began to retract into the stone. "You're good to go," he said as Elroy continued forwards.

He moved towards the roar of industrial machinery until he found several large digging machines. They were big, with a drill on the front, which was wider than he was tall. The two digging machines were silent and pointed towards a dark, narrow passage, down which he heard more drilling. Then, finally, somebody broke off from a conversation and hurried toward him. "Thank goodness you're here! I assume you're here to fix the machines, yes?" said the man. He wore a bright yellow hardhat and talked excitedly. Elroy nodded. "Okay, well, it's the one over there, on the left," he said. And he continued talking as they walked. "Thank the lord you're here. I have a quota to meet, y'know? And with one of the diggers offline, it'd been a challenge, not that it isn't any way," he finished as they reached the problem machine.

The diagnosis wasn't a problem. Within seconds Elroy knew the problem. A necessary pipe had burst, and the supervisor said that high-pressure steam shot out of the pipe when they tried to turn it on. He set down his duffel, withdrew a welder and mask, and began to work. The supervisor, however, kept jabbering, "You've no idea how hard it's been. I mean, when I was told to excavate a collapsed tunnel, I thought it would be easier. Not easy, but easier than this!" He said, gesturing vaguely to his surroundings. "The tunnels are so thin, the diggers can barely fit through! And when you think you're making good progress, you find a bit of the tunnel has flooded, and just.. Argh!" the supervisor continued. Then he stomped off in frustration to shout at one of his workers.

After welding the pipe, he fixed another series of minor problems and was out of there in just a few hours. Once he exited the elevator, he walked around for a few minutes. He walked around the plaza. People had set up shops throughout where you could buy all sorts of stuff you didn't need. Finally, he moved towards the fountain in the center of the plaza. He sat on the rim of the fountain, watching the crowds of people. He thought about how each of these people had a life of their own. How they were each living a life he knew nothing about. Actually, he knew a few people who passed by, they'd wave, and he'd wave back. After some time, he checked his watch and realized that he was behind. He hopped up and walked back to his workplace. Not surprisingly, Tobias had already returned and lounged on a chair near the door. "that was quick," he said as Elroy shed his duffel bag. "I could say the same thing to you," Elroy replied.

"What can I say? I've gotten good at fixing lamps" Tobias shrugged. "Seeing as we're both done early, wanna grab some lunch?" he added. "Sure," Elroy said as he dropped off his heavy toolbelt. He and Tobias were good friends, had been for years. And he didn't think he would handle the loss of his father so well without him, that and his work to focus on. "Y'know, it still doesn't feel like he's gone," Elroy said while eating sandwiches. "Well, I felt the same when I lost my childhood dog," Tobias said. "Is this the same childhood dog you found two weeks later?" Elroy said. Tobias dismissed this with a wave of his hand. "You know what I mean," he said.

"The funeral is today," Tobias said after a long pause. "I know," Elroy said; Tobias let it drop.

Dome Eight had a small cemetery tucked away outside the heart of the city. The cemetery was one of the only spots with any significant amount of dirt and grass beside the park. The area was laden with headstones, and another one had just been installed. There weren't a lot of people there. Among them was Tobias, the red-headed girl, and the lunch lady whose name seemed to change each time he asked. They all wore black, or as much black as they had; some wore black pants or a black hat, but the theme was clear. A priest was there, he said some words that Elroy didn't hear, and the closed casket was lowered into the grave with frightening finality.

He hurried home after that, not wanting to talk to anyone. He sat alone in silence for a while until he heard a knock on his door. All his energy had been drained. He almost didn't get up from the couch. But after a second, a more impatient knock shook the door he lifted himself from the comfort of his couch. He opened the door, expecting Tobias. But instead, it was a young paperboy carrying a small box. He was young. He looked as if he had only just entered puberty. "I was told to deliver this to you, sir. Sorry for your loss" he handed the box to Elroy and stood in the doorway awkwardly. Elroy fished around his pocket and withdrew a few dollar bills "Thanks!" The boy said. He turned, mounted his bicycle, and pedaled off. Elroy closed the door and examined the box. It was made out of cheap, probably recycled cardboard. Inside the box were a letter and a bunch of seemingly random items. The letter told him that the things inside the box were what his father had on him when he was found. Elroy didn't know where. Inside the box was the kind of thing you'd expect, a pocket watch, pen, that kind of thing. But it was what wasn't there that gave him pause. He set the box down and searched the apartment. He opened all the cabinets and drawers in the kitchen, lifted the couch cushions, he searched the bedroom, but nothing.

Chapter 3

It was before the Flood when he was less than a year old. And he was at his parents' wedding. After they were pronounced husband and wife, their joy was so much that it spilled over onto him, even though he had no way of knowing what was happening. His parents, Andrew and Elise, had dragged him in front of a camera. The bride was still in her wedding dress, and the groom was still in his tuxedo that matched his son's. The picture was black and white, but his father had cherished it. He kept it with him at all times, he slept with it, he took it to work, wherever he was, the picture was, and it wasn't in the box, and it wasn't in the house.

While searching the bedroom, he had the mind to search under the mattress. And while he didn't find the picture, he did find something else that piqued his interest.

It was a torn piece of paper with weird symbols written on it. What was odd was that Elroy recognized it. He didn't know from where or what it meant, but he was determined to find out. He was thinking about this when his stomach dropped as he heard the sirens, the worst sound imaginable. The loud wailing filled his mind, and he quickly took the paper from where he had found it, stuffed it into his pocket, and sprinted out the door like his life depended on it because it did. When he left the apartment, he saw a flood of people running away from their homes and toward the city center.

When he arrived, there was a man dressed in uniform. He was shouting instructions into a megaphone. Four groups of people descended into four different hatches, all equidistant from the fountain's center of the plaza. The lines were long, and almost everyone rushed to get into the shelters. And Elroy was the last in line. His turn to climb down was approaching. The city darkened, and all non-essential systems and lights were disabled. His heart began to beat faster, if that was possible, as he saw a *huge* black shape glide across the top of the dome. It was bigger than all the most prominent buildings in the city combined, easily covering a third of the dome. The last thing he heard before descending down the hatch was the loud and ominous thud as something beat against the glass before the hatch slammed shut.

He found himself in near-complete darkness,

but he could hear masses of people breathing, shuffling, and whispering. When his eyes adjusted to the dim, red emergency lighting, he found himself on a small spiral staircase. He slowly began to walk down the stairs. First, he had to wait for the person in front of him to move, and then he would take their place. It took a few minutes for everyone to reach the shelter proper, but not nearly as long as he thought it would've taken, given how many people there were. The main room was separated from the staircase by a large metal door, which was currently open. The room itself was a large concrete square. The back wall was lined with shelving that held rations and survival equipment. They all stood together, a quarter of the city's population shoulder to shoulder.

He could hear nothing except for the breathing and whispering of the people around him and the sound of the HVAC keeping them alive.

If the shelter flooded, there was another sealed level to retreat to. And in case that one also flooded, there was a third level to flee to. Though no matter how safe the residents were, Elroy felt horrible, the stress tying his stomach in knots. Thankfully after only an hour or two, one of the uniformed men moved towards the big, metal door. He looked through the peephole on the door. After a few moments, he concluded that the outer room hadn't flooded. With the help of a few nearby citizens, he opened the heavy door. It closed with a clang behind him. Within a few minutes, he returned, announcing that everybody was okay and they could leave. Slowly, everyone exited the shelter. He scanned the roof as soon as he clambered off the staircase and into the plaza. Thankfully, it seemed undamaged, bar a single leak gushing water, but emergency crews had already been dispatched. If he squinted, he could see a few of them suspended from the dome by long ropes. Elroy spotted Tobias as he was with his parents. He gave each of them a quick hug. He then spotted Elroy, who then ran towards him. "Wow, that was scary," Tobias said. "Yeah, I'm glad that we're okay," Elroy said. Tobias' parents called him back over. "See you later!" Tobias said, walking away. Elroy waved and then began the long walk home. As he approached his apartment, he was glad that it was on the ground floor, as all his energy evaporated when he got home. He climbed onto his bunk and quickly fell asleep.

Chapter 4

He got up early, sat at his dining table, and examined the paper. The symbols looked strange. He recognized them but did not know from where. It looked like a language, and he didn't know from which deep recess in his mind it came from, but he recognized one of the words, secret. He and Tobias were at their usual hangout spot, the pawnshop. He showed the paper to Tobias, who had the same confused reaction as he had. "Yeah, I have no idea what that is," Tobias said with a shrug. "But what's even weirder is that I know what this word means, secret," Elroy said. "Oh! Now we're talking!" said Tobias, his interest renewed. "So if you can read that word, then what is it? Sure isn't English," Tobias said. "That's the weirdest part of this all, I don't know," Elroy said. "What you guys talkin' about?" said the girl who worked the pawnshop, Patrice.

She was about his age, and she had long curly red hair and an extra helping of freckles. "Elroy found this strange piece of paper under his dad's mattress," Tobias said, waving the paper at her. She moved from behind the counter and pulled one of the old chairs the pawnshop sold to their equally old table. "Lemme see," Patrice said, reaching for the paper. Tobias handed it to her. "Be careful," Elroy said as Patrice scanned the document. She snapped her fingers, trying to remember something. "Y'know what? I recognize the language, but from where?" she said, scratching her scalp. After a few moments, her eyes widened, and she rushed out of the room, and they could hear her sorting through the junk. After a good few minutes, she returned with a large wooden sign that looked like it would hang outside an old-timey tavern, it went down to her knees, and she could barely fit her arms around it. As soon she entered the room, Elroy rushed to help her, and together they sat it face-up on the floor. The words on the sign were written in the same script like the ones on the paper, although they clearly said different things. "You've no idea how much old crap I had to wade through to find this," she said proudly as she sat back down. "What is it?" Said Tobias. "I don't know," she said, shrugging. "But it's a good start," she added. They all stared at the sign, hoping it would somehow translate itself. When such a thing failed to happen, Elroy said, "Well, who sold it?" "That's a good question, but I don't know how far back the logs go. I could check, though," she said. She left again, this time for less than a minute, and returned with a huge book that rattled the table when she dropped it. They looked through that book for a while, and after all that time, all they learned was that it wasn't bought in the last ten years. "Welp," Tobias said as he stood and dusted his hands, "I say we break for lunch" "Agreed," Patrice said as she pushed back her chair.

Tobias suggested that they go to the same sandwich place they always do. But Patrice wanted to go to her favorite restaurant, a noodle place pretty close to the pawnshop. So they turned to Elroy, and he voted for the noodles.

Patrice ate her portion with chopsticks and much more precision than Elroy, who clumsily squeezed the noodles. Finally, he looked over at Tobias, who had long since given up and asked for a fork. Tobias and Patrice had finished their meals and waited for him to finish. "C'mon, man, just use a fork," said Tobias. "I think the chopsticks add to the experience," said Patrice. "I don't care about the 'experience'; I just want to eat and leave," replied Tobias. Eventually, Elroy finished his meal, and they headed outside. They all flopped down on a bench. They sat in silence for a little while before Patrice spoke. "Hey, if you don't mind, I got to run some errands," Patrice said as she stood. "We could come with you. It's not like we're doing anything else," Elroy said as he looked at Tobias, who shrugged. "Oh, okay then. Come with me," she said as she began to walk down the street.

She led them to a nondescript, gray building that neither Tobias nor Elroy had ever been to but still feared, the archives office. The place reeked of old people, stale air, and dead dreams. The switchback queues took forever for Patrice to get to the desk at the end, while Tobias and Elroy sat on some chairs lining one of the walls. "Why'd you volunteer us for this?" said Tobias. "I don't know. I didn't think she'd take us to the most boring place on earth," said Elroy. It took the better part of an hour, but Patrice finally reached the desk. Where an old woman handed her a key with a number on it. Patrice thanked her and waved Tobias and Elroy over as she walked through a side door. The door led into a long hallway with many doors splitting off it. "That took so long!" said Tobias as they caught up. "Actually, that was rather quick," said Patrice. "That was fast?" said Tobias. "How often have you been to the archives?" asked Elroy. "Actually, quite often, my dad, although he owns a pawn shop, is an up-and-coming engineer. So he has me fetch records and blueprints from all over the place. And plus, I quite like it here. It's fun learning about what happened leading up to the Flood," Patrice answered.

They stopped after not too much walking when they reached a door labeled 1949. Patrice inserted the key the clerk had given her. The door creaked open, and they walked inside. The room was circular. And the walls were lined with large filing cabinets. As Patrice began rummaging around, Tobias sat against the door, and Elroy wandered around the room.

The door they came through was ajar, and Elroy decided to wander around the hallway. After a few minutes of pacing back and forth, Elroy noticed a gray door with a padlock. More so than his curiosity, his boredom compelled him to ask, "Hey, what's behind this door?" A few seconds later, Patrice poked her head out of the room. "I don't know, but whatever it is, we can't go inside," she said, standing next to him. "I wonder what's inside," said Elroy. "Probably just maintenance or something," Patrice said, shrugging. "Well, let's find out," Tobias said, rummaging through his backpack. He withdrew a rusty pair of bolt cutters. "Why do you have bolt cutters with you?" Said Patrice, "Always keep 'em with me. Never know when you'll need to cut something."

Tobias said, patting the bolt cutters. He moved to the door when Elroy stopped him. "What do you think you're doing?" he said. "Opening the door," Tobias said. "I'm not sure that's a good idea," Patrice said. "What they don't know won't hurt them," Tobias said. "What they don't know? It'll be clear as day that we did it," Patrice said. "Yeah, man, I don't know if that's the best plan," Elroy said. "I'd rather not," Patrice said. Her frustration grew when she heard the snap of the padlock breaking. "Oops, my hands slipped," said Tobias grinning. Patrice, visibly upset, walked away, trying to control her frustration. "Well, if we're going to get caught, might as well see what's inside," said Elroy. Although frustrated, Patrice's curiosity got the better of her, and she entered the room with them. They entered the dark room, leaving the door ajar behind them. At first, she thought she was right, that this was some kind of maintenance tunnel. But when Tobias withdrew a flashlight, she realized she was wrong. The narrow beam of light swept over rows of file cabinets. "Guess it's not maintenance," Tobias said, wielding the flashlight.

Following Tobias, they explored the room. It was larger than it seemed, with several rows of file cabinets. Not all of them were labeled. Very few were, but one caught Patrice's eye. It was labeled 'U-2 Incident' Patrice stopped and stared at the cabinet while the boys moved on. In her studies and her time in the archives, she'd seen many references to the U-2 but had no idea of its history. She hadn't been able to find anything on it until now. Tobias and Elroy noticed that she'd stopped and turned and "What're you looking at?" Elroy asked. Patrice had pulled open one of the cabinet drawers and rummaged around in it. "Something called the 'U-2 Incident,'" she said. "What's a U-2?" Elroy asked as they returned to Patrice." I've no idea; that's why I'm interested," she said.

Elroy and Tobias sat down and began leafing through files. Eventually, Patrice grabbed the flashlight and started reading the file in her hands. Her eyes bulged as she read. She held up a finger to silence the unrelated conversation between Elroy and Tobias; she had to reread the lines out loud. "'A Lockheed U-2 spy plane was shot down near Sverdlovsk, and its pilot captured. The Soviets salvaged enough of the craft's surveillance equipment

imagined Tobias being disciplined, his parents shouting at him, and he would be bored. He would never get it, would he? His actions have consequences, and the rules are there for a reason, no matter how dumb that reason was. He went to his bedroom, climbing over the empty lower bunk and into the higher one.

They reconvened at the pawnshop the next day. Patrice leaned against the counter, looking worried, while Tobias sat at their old table, looking frustrated. Upon entering, he knew who he wanted to talk to. "What's wrong?" He said as he sat down on a stool he pulled next to the counter.

"Well... it's just. My dad is currently applying for an important position. He said he didn't want me to ruin it by causing a ruckus," she said.

"What about you?" Elroy said to Tobias. "I'm being punished unfairly," he blurted out. "One more time, they said, and I'd be grounded for a month!" He said.

After a while, they noticed that nobody had entered the shop today. So he and Tobias suggested they hang out somewhere that smelled less like mold. Patrice hesitated, but she agreed when they both promised to buy something later.

They quickly ruled out both Patrice and Tobias' houses. So they ended up crammed into Elroy's three-room apartment. Elroy and Patrice were sitting on the couch, while Tobias was sitting in a nearby armchair. After a few seconds of silence, "What now?" asked Tobias. They both shrugged. After thinking a few more moments, Tobias said, "I know; what about hide and seek?" Elroy answered, "You've got to be kidding." "Well, what else are we going to do?" said Patrice. "Fine," Elroy said with a sigh. "Y'know, if you really wanted to play hide and seek, we could have gone to the park," said Elroy as Tobias closed his eyes, and he and Patrice scurried off to find somewhere to hide.

When he opened his eyes, Tobias was somewhat surprised he couldn't already see them. He looked near where they sat. The couch and armchair with a small coffee table in between. On a whim, he looked beneath the furniture, nothing, though that was a stretch. He moved to the other side of the room, where the stove and cabinets were. He stood there more a moment, considering if one of them could fit inside one of the lower cabinets. He opened one, it was empty, and he decided it was too small. He opened the door to the tiny bathroom. A quick glance was all he needed to confirm no one was there. The entrance to the bedroom was opposite the kitchen, and he opened it. The bunk beds are in the corner by the door and the window on the far wall. Now, this was what he was expecting. Elroy was clearly not committed to hiding and stood behind the extremely thin, almost floor-length curtains. Tobias could see him and vice versa. But he feigned not being able to see Elroy. He examined the bunk beds and even lifted up the picture on the wall to see if he was behind it. But Tobias wasn't mindful of the frame, and when he lifted the picture frame to check underneath it, the frame hit the floor and shattered. Elroy's heart skipped a beat when it began to fall. He brushed the curtain aside and examined the picture. The picture itself was intact. He was happy about that. It was a picture of his mom, dad, and him, though not the one that his dad kept with him. But the frame was ruined. Tobias began furiously apologizing.

Hearing a noise from the kitchen, Elroy looked through the open door to see Patrice.

It was unsettling to see her unfurl herself as she struggled out of one of the small cabinets. "What happened?" She said once she was free.

"Oh," she said once she saw the shattered glass

on the floor. "Don't worry about it. Just the frame broke," Elroy said. "But that looked like a nice frame," Tobias said. "Well... yeah," Elroy looking at his feet. Patrice put her arm around Elroy's shoulder. "Don't worry about it. I'm sure there's a nice frame somewhere in the pawnshop. I'll even give you a discount," she said with a smile. "Um, guys," Tobias said, pointing to the spot on the wall where the picture used to hang. There were a few Russian characters carved on the wall. "Woah," said Elroy. "You don't happen to know what that says, do you?" Said Patrice. "No clue," Elroy. He went into the living room and returned with a pen and a small piece of paper. He transcribed the text onto the paper. "Let's find someone who does," Elroy said.

"I know just the person," said Patrice. She led them a few blocks. "She lives in a large house but spends most of her time on her porch smoking cigars. According to her, she and her husband live there. But nobody has seen him in years. So most people assumed he was fake, or something happened to him" was all the information Patrice provided about this person. Finally, they approached a fancy-looking house much more substantial than any of their homes. Elroy wondered how she could afford a house like that. There was a woman on the porch. She was old; she looked like she was pushing seventy. She was relatively thin and had a walking cane next to her wooden rocking chair.

As the trio approached the porch, Patrice waved. "Well, if it isn't Patrice!" she said as they climbed the few steps onto the porch. "And who are your friends?" She said. "This is Elroy," Patrice said as Elroy waved. "And this is Tobias" Tobias nodded. "It's nice to meet you, boys. I'm Auntie Mable," She said. "Sit down, sit down," she said, gesturing toward a bench. "Now, what do you need?" She said once they had sat down. "Can I not just come to see you?" Patrice said. "Yes, you could, though I'm not sure you would," Auntie Mable said with a chuckle. "Okay, you're right. We need to talk to someone who speaks Russian," Patrice said.

"Hmmm," Auntie Mable said while taking a drag from her cigar. "That's a tough one. Not many people speak it. And those who do hide it well," she said. After a few seconds, she continued, "He might not be the most hospitable, but ol' Captain Morozov might be able to help," She said. "I can write that down for you if you want?" She said.

Elroy handed her the paper with the Russian on

it and a pen. She wrote something on the other side of the paper. Then, she handed the paper back to Elroy, and it had Emrik Morozov and an address on it. "Thank you so much, Auntie," Patrice said. Patrice moved toward Auntie Mable and gave her a kiss on either cheek. "Your welcome, my dear," she said as they walked away. As they walked away, Elroy turned towards Patrice. "Are you related?" He asked. "Nope," Patrice answered.

Chapter 6

After another good few minutes of walking, they reached the address Auntie Mable gave them. They saw it was a large apartment complex, where they entered the dirty and rundown lobby. They tried to buzz the apartment on the intercom. But while it had a list of all the apartments, one was missing. The nameplate has been aggressively removed, and the button equally so. "Looks like this guy doesn't want to be bothered," said Patrice. "Yeah, but let's go bother him anyway!" said Tobias, already heading for the stairs. "I don't know if that's the best idea," Patrice said, but he'd already begun climbing the stairs. She and Elroy reluctantly followed.

Once they reached his door, they found the number had been sanded off and replaced with a string of profanities suggesting that they should leave. "Do we really need to talk to him?" asked Elroy, "I mean, it's just some words," Tobias said.

"Yeah, but very mean words," Elroy said. "Surely we'd be able to find someone else more personable who speaks Russian," Patrice said.

Tobias knocked on the door, not

acknowledging their complaints. "C'mon, man, every time," Elroy muttered.

After a few seconds, a scratchy voice called, "What'd you want!" Elroy took a deep breath and said," I need to talk to you" "Why?" The voice said. "I need you to translate something, пожалуйста," Said Elroy stumbling over what he was pretty sure was please in Russian.

After a long few moments, the voice responded, "y'know kid, your pronunciation is horrific" He heard the sound of a deadbolt unlocking, and then the door swung open. He must have been Emrik; the man was quite large, at least six feet tall. He had an equally large, unkempt, gray beard. But for all the hair on his face, he was lacking on his head, which was almost entirely bald. And it was apparent he hadn't left the house or showered for at least a few weeks. When he opened the door jumped a little "Christ, there are three of ya," he said. "Sorry about that," Elroy said. He stood in the doorway, pondering. "You can come in, but not your friends," he said. Elroy looked back, nervous. Then, with silent worry from Patrice and Tobias' look of impending boredom, he went inside. The two entered the apartment. And when the door closed, all the light went with it. Elroy heard him fumbling around in the dark before lighting a lantern. As the room brightened, he saw just how messy it was. Clothes and empty packaging coating everything. He swept an arm across the couch, removing most of the mess, and motioned for Elroy to sit.

"So, you said you needed something translated?" Erik said. The way the light played on his face made him look quite menacing. He hesitated when he responded, "Well, it's kind of a long story, but I found these words scratched into my wall" "That's pretty weird, let me see," Emrik said, and Elroy handed him the paper. "Hmm, that's ominous," he said. "What does it say," Elroy said eagerly. "It says 'I'm alive', and this is an address," he said. Elroy's heart skipped a beat as hope flooded him, but he tried to keep it in check. "Thanks," Elroy said. He moved to leave but turned back. "Y'know before I got here, I was told you'd be much less inviting and grumpier, no offense," Elroy said. "So you're wondering what happened? And why do I live alone in a dark apartment lit by a single gas lamp?" Emrik asked. Elroy nodded. "Well, for that, you'll have to sit back down" Emrik stood and walked to the kitchen, "And I'm going to need a beer."

"It all started before the flood. I bet you barely remember it if you were alive back then. Anyways, I was a fantastic submarine captain, cream of the crop, best of the best. But that was part of the problem. See, I sunk so many American subs; before the war went nuclear, when my time was up and my quarters were flooding, and my crew was drowning, it was my undoing. We were sinking; our enemy had a scratch barely, so I did what any reasonable soul would do; I surrendered. But within only a few days, I began to regret my decision, as I was to be executed.

The few days I spent in that prison were horrible, not because the conditions were terrible, I mean they were, but because I knew I was waiting for my death. I was taken from my cell, and I was certain I would be shot, but instead, I was taken to an office, sat down, and offered a job. Apparently, some higher up, who I never got to thank, had decided that I was more valuable alive than dead. I was to serve as a submarine captain again, only this time for the United States. I agreed on two conditions. That all my remaining crew was to be released, back home. And more importantly, at least to me, was that my wife was to move to the States to live with me. They agreed reluctantly. And I was back to sinking submarines, but this time I would shed a tear each time one sank. Now, me and the Americans didn't get along all the time. But for the most part, it was smooth sailing. That was until both sides started slinging nukes at each other. Hell, I contributed to the hellfire. My submarine was armed with a single warhead, and I was obligated to fire it, and I did. Don't worry, I hit Siberia. I'm sure no one died. Anyways, I was accused of being a spy. And while there was no evidence, it still took me down a peg. But I was still quite high ranking, so I was guaranteed a spot in the network of domes hidden deep underwater. And so was my wife. But there was a horrible bureaucratic accident, and we were separated. But this was, at least I was told, not uncommon, and many loved ones were separated. But thankfully, all the domes were interconnected. And they'd sent her over any day now. Yes, I was angry, but it was okay; she'd be here any day, right? Well no. The first load of people came through the pneumatic line; they were met with a lot of fanfare. But then the tunnel collapsed, and everyone on the second bus was killed. Don't worry, my dear wife was scheduled for the third. We kept in touch somewhat by sending letters via messenger submarines. But when the submarines started disappearing, we stopped, and I've not spoken to her in damn near five years! Can you imagine! They said these domes were meant to last lifetimes! But within the first year, the veins were severed! Have you ever wondered about food shortages? The strict rationing that has been going on for the last decade? Well, that was Dome Two; they had the expansive farms and cattle. I told them it was a stupid idea to specialize the domes! Sorry, can you tell I've not spoken to anybody in a while? Anyway, I was in this dome, alone. And I went into a downward spiral. And eventually, I was fired, for showing up late, for not showing up at all. And when I did, I was angry, hungover, and a rusty captain. And now I've been living off the meager benefits they gave me."

Elroy looked stunned, "Umm, sorry about the ranting, it is just-" Emrik started. "No, it's fine. I'm just surprised," Elroy said. "I know, I should really see a shrink," Emrik said with a chuckle. Then, with some thank yous and goodbyes, Elroy left.

When he exited the apartment, he saw Patrice and Tobias slumped against the wall on either side of the door. "What took you so long?" Tobias said, "He had a lot to say," said Elroy with a shrug. "Did he translate it?" Asked Patrice. Elroy checked to make sure no one was in the hall. "It says, 'I'm alive', and this is an address," Elroy whispered. "Is it..." Tobias said, letting the question ask itself. "I don't know," Elroy said. "Welp, only one way to find out," Patrice said with a light slap on Elroy's back.

Chapter 7

The address was on the other side of the city. And was on the wrong side of town. They were lucky it was still bright, but they still had to dodge a few thugs. And they argued over whether they saw someone getting mugged. When they finally arrived at the address, they were... disappointed. It was a small abandoned storefront; the windows and door were boarded up. "Is that it?" Tobias said. They stood on the sidewalk, looking at the building. "I guess we're going in then," Elroy said. "Really?" Tobias said, "How?" Asked Patrice. Elroy turned to Tobias. "Yes, really," he looks at Patrice. "I'm going to pry off the boards," he said. "With what?" She asked. He rummaged around in his tool belt, which he carried around just in case, and withdrew his hammer. It took a considerable effort. Elroy prying with the hammer, and Tobias helping pull them off. Patrice watched, afraid she'd cut herself with a rusty nail, which in fairness, did almost happen to both of them. Once a few boards were removed, just enough to force the rusty door open, Elroy produced a flashlight and crept through the door with Tobias and Patrice in tow. It was very dark and creepy, something Patrice pointed out multiple times, Elroy agreed, but the single room was empty. "Damn, just empty shelves," Tobias said. "Same over here," said Elroy. "Oh well, guess I have to leave the creepy abandoned store," said Patrice, but she was stopped when Tobias said, "Toss me the flashlight; I think I see something" Elroy did precisely that. Tobias caught it and aimed the beam near the floor, towards the back of the building. "You see this?" He said Elroy walked over and saw a bit of the floor was wooden; instead of the tile that was in the rest of the store. "I think this bit of shelf is covering something," Tobias said. Elroy and Tobias gave it a quick shove, but they needed Patrice's help, and she reluctantly agreed. The three of them made quick work of moving the shelf a foot, revealing a trapdoor built into the floor. Tobias handed the flashlight to Elroy. "You first," he said. "What!? Are you guys really going to go down a trapdoor into the basement of a dark store just because some weird cryptic message was carved into your wall!?" Patrice said, hands on her hips. They looked at each other, then both at Patrice; they nodded. "I guess that means I'm going too," she said. "Guess so," Tobias said as he kneeled and wrenched open the trapdoor. The trapdoor revealed pitch black. And when Elroy aimed the flashlight down, he saw a set of stairs so steep they were almost a ladder. "Good luck," Said Tobias. "I mean, it's probably an empty, boring basement, right?" Elroy said, "Sure," Tobias said as Elroy eased himself down the trapdoor and onto the stairs. The stairs were relatively short, and once he hopped down onto the landing, the first thing he noticed was how cramped it was. Elroy didn't know how he knew this. He hadn't had a chance to sweep the flashlight across the room yet. But he just knew; it felt like the walls were close. And his suspicion was proved true once he illuminated the room. It was small and looked to be some sort of workshop. With a stool and several work tables taking up the majority of the space and a large bulletin board covering the majority of one wall. "You can come down now!" He shouted up. A minute later, they were all staring in awe at the desks. They were covered in designs and plans that, at a glance, made no sense to him. The bulletin board was covered with maps, coordinates, and frequencies. But the thing that drew his attention was a dusty, unopened letter sitting on the middle desk, right in front of the stool. "What does any of this mean?" Patrice said, drifting around the room. "Well, it seems to be plans for...

something," Tobias said, leafing through hand-drawn designs. They noticed that Elroy was silent and saw him staring at the letter. "What's that?" Asked Patrice, moving to his side. "I don't know," he said. He reached out and gingerly picked it up, leaving a square absent of dust. Unlike most of the paper here, which had a slight tinge of decay, the letter, other than dust, was pristine. "Are you going to open it?" She said. Elroy slid his finger into the crease in the paper, breaking the seal.

Chapter 8

Dear Elroy

I hope this letter finds you well. And, I'm sorry this is how I had to tell you. But, as you've probably figured out by now, I've left. I'm not dead, at least at the time of writing, but I have a feeling they'd cover it up. My guess is that I'll have a funeral. The people of this dome like to jump to conclusions. I assume you're reading this in my secret workshop? Sorry about hiding that as well, but if so, look at the board. You should see coordinates and radio frequencies. And I know nobody uses radio anymore, outside the dome at least. But that's where these radio signals were coming from, the deep blue. I detected multiple signals. They all said different things, sometimes in morse code, sometimes in English, sometimes in other languages. But they were all getting across the same point; they needed help.

So, in short, that's where I've gone. To find the source of these, hopefully, automated distress signals. And if all goes to plan, you may never read this, as my lowest estimate says I'll only be gone for a week or two. But you know me, I'm not really an optimist. So it might take me months, though I hope it does not. I'm so sorry I had to hide all this from you. But I couldn't risk people finding out about all this.

*And one more thing, DO NOT COME
LOOKING FOR ME.*
Love, Dad

"Oh my," whispered Patrice, who Elroy had
forgotten was reading over his shoulder.

"What?" Tobias said. When he saw that they
were reading a letter, "let me see," he said. Elroy
hesitated but handed the letter over.

"Woah," he said once he had finished reading
it. Then, after a few moments of silence, "What
now?" Said Tobias. "Well, we go looking for him,"
Elroy said. "But he said not to," Patrice said. "I know,
but he's alive, and he could be in danger," Elroy said.
"We?" "Well, I assumed that you'd help me find my
dad, who until very recently I thought was dead,"
Elroy said. "When you put it like that," Tobias said
with a chuckle.

"Um, how would we go about that, finding
him?" Patrice said. "I've no idea," Elroy said. "Okay,
what about if we put this on hold for now and come
back here tomorrow?" Patrice said. "It's not late. Why
would we stop now?" Elroy said. "Well, if I'm being
honest, this all hurts my brain, and it's all happening
pretty quick," Patrice said. "I agree; all this thinking is

making me hungry," Tobias said. "Okay, we'll come back tomorrow," Elroy said with a sigh.

They returned with some furniture the next day to make the dark, cold, and uncomfortable workshop a little more bearable. Patrice pulled a wagon behind her with an armchair in it. While Elroy and Tobias carried a folded couch on their shoulders. When they got to the door, they managed to fit the couch in, but the chair proved difficult, but after some squeezing, they got it through. The trapdoor, though, was a different story. They managed to get the couch down with a lot of finesse, but no matter how much they tried, the armchair just wouldn't fit. So, Patrice ended up sitting on the old stool already down there. Elroy looked at the silver lining; the old armchair smelled like cigarettes. They also found the cord that turned on the single lightbulb on the roof. "So... how are we going to get out of the dome?" Asked Elroy, "That's the big question," Patrice said. "Not just that, we also need a submarine," Tobias said as he stood and walked to the bulletin board. "These coordinates are way out of diving suit distance" he sat back down but didn't stop talking. "And if we're going to use a submarine, then we need rations, spare filters, and, like, a pilot," Tobias finished. "Wow, that's some hard stuff to get," Patrice said.

"Well, let's start with the hardest; how do we get a submarine?" Said Elroy. "We could sign up for patrols, then take off instead of patrolling?" Tobias suggested. "Yeah, but to do that, you need to take submarine training, which can take months if not years," said Elroy. "Also, if we just take off, it'll be very unsubtle, and we'll get in an astronomical amount of trouble," Patrice added. "Look, we're going to steal a submarine. Let's not worry about getting into trouble," Tobias said. "Steal is a strong word," said Elroy. "Well, how else are we going to get a submarine?" Said Tobias. "I don't know," said Elroy. "Wait, you remember the flood that happened last year?" Asked Patrice, "Remember it? We had to clean it up," said Tobias, gesturing to himself and Elroy. "Well, a portion of the submarine pens were trashed. But because our shrinking fleet of submarines were already struggling to fill the space, they just sealed a portion of the pens off, they drained it but left it destroyed." Said Patrice. "So, you're saying we should search the abandoned pens just in case someone left behind a submarine?" Asked Elroy. "It couldn't hurt," said Patrice.

As they walked towards the pens, they quickly

entered a different part of town, the part of town where all the important people lived. It was significantly fancier than where they lived. The houses all had a fresh coat of paint, the sidewalks were clear of litter, and there was substantially less grime than anywhere else. There weren't many people walking around, but the few who were out were smartly dressed and walked like they had somewhere to be. They often had to dodge people on the street. Not because they weren't allowed here, they were just walking down the road, but because people would start asking questions. They could have gotten disguises if they had thought about it a bit more. And all it would be is to take a shower and put on some fancier clothes. Unfortunately, none of them could afford fancy clothes. Despite their dodging, someone did ask them where they were going. Elroy had the foresight to bring his toolbox, which he hoisted and said they were on their way to repair something. They hurried off before he could ask what or why Patrice was with them, as Tobias also looked ready to fix something. They eventually reached a section that was cordoned off with yellow tape. They ducked beneath the tape and quickly moved onwards. This relatively small part of the dome was abandoned after a sizable leak in the dome. Recently a few work crews had begun work to restore this part of town, but they were easily snuck past. They found the pens soon afterward. They passed an abandoned pair of guard posts, and through a large door they all three had to lift to get past, it made a loud bang as it fell back to the floor, and they were plunged into darkness. Elroy fumbled around, eventually turning on his flashlight. He then produced two more and handed them out. The three beams of light pierced the darkness, surveying their surroundings. They were stood on a wide walkway. On their right was a tall wall lined with empty crates and dollies. On their left were the individual submarine pens. It had only been like this for a year, yet there were algae *everywhere*. "Wow," Elroy said as they started to move forwards. "It's very humid in here," said Patrice. "So, what are we looking for?" Asked Tobias. "I dunno, a submarine, I guess," said Elroy. They walked further. "It's pretty scary," said Patrice. Elroy agreed but wasn't about to say anything.

"It's a lot louder than I thought it would be," she continued. "Well, we're right up against the edge of the dome," said Elroy, explaining the loud creaking and groaning of the walls around them. "Guys!

Guys!" Shouted Tobias pointing into one of the pens. Inside, it was the perfect submarine. It was large but still small enough to be operated by three people. It also had large rail guns and torpedo tubes." Woah," said Elroy. "It's perfect," said Tobias proudly. "Umm, sorry to burst your bubble, but it's got some serious damage," noted Elroy. "Nothing a little elbow grease can't fix," added Tobias, scanning the hull with his flashlight. "No, like half the tail is missing," said Elroy. "Looks like more than half," Patrice added.

They were disappointed, but they continued on; however, this letdown became a regular occurrence. They would find a promising submarine in the search, only to find out it was abandoned with good reason. This happened four or five times until they found one with no external damage, at least that they could see. "Really? This is the submarine that's not damaged!" Said Tobias.

It was a black tube with a finned tower on top. It was small for a submarine; just two people probably could have operated it, or one very determined and skilled person.

It was about eighty feet long. It looked like a messenger submarine, and as such, it would have no armaments, though its engine should be up to scratch.

"It's tiny!" Said Tobias. "Well, it's better than swimming," said Elroy. There was silence for a few moments. "So," Elroy said, looking at his companions, "Are we going to go inside or what?" Patrice declined, sighting her fear of small spaces which may flood at any minute. Tobias pointed out that if they were going to go for real, then that would be a problem. Patrice said that she'd figure it out once they got there. So Elroy lowered himself down the hatch, with only Tobias following. It was very dark and smelled very bad. It smelled so strongly of mold that he had to stop mid-way down the ladder to catch his breath. Once they were in the submarine proper, they found it was empty and decrepit. At the front was the pilot's room, it had a lot of panels and buttons that they had no clue as to their function, but the chair looked comfy once the mold was removed. Behind that was a room with four bunk beds currently folded against the walls. Further back were the storage and engine room. They exited out the bunk room, out the hatch. "It smells so bad in there," said Tobias as they exited the submarine. "Well, I'm glad I stayed here," said Patrice. "It's small and gross, but it is watertight," said Elroy once they'd grouped up again. 'So... is that it? Do we have a submarine now?' Asked Patrice.

"Well, yes, but though it's watertight, it still needs some fixing up. Nothing me and Tobias can't do. But then there's the problem of getting it out of the pen and into the water," said Elroy. "We'll cross that bridge when we get to it," Tobias said as they walked back to the entrance. "So now what?" Patrice asked. "I don't know, diving suits, I guess," Elroy said.

Chapter 9

They returned to the workshop and began brainstorming. The group could, in theory, buy them, but they were ludicrously expensive. And so, when no one could come up with a better idea, they decided to steal some. While they technically were going to steal a submarine, none of them felt bad about stealing a rusting, abandoned submarine. But they were hesitant to actually steal something. They came up with a plan that was not great. But hopefully, it will work.

Earlier that day, Tobias raided the janitorial closet and pushed a cart filled with cleaning supplies. Unfortunately, he was wearing a uniform a size too big. He walked side by side with Patrice as they entered the aquarium. It was the nicest place in the dome, which was open to the public at least. It hugged the edge of the dome, and as well as seeing fish in tanks, you could also peer out into the ocean.

And most importantly for them, they also did tours of the nearby seafloor. Nobody stopped Tobias and Patrice as they walked through the aquarium. They reached the tour room with no incident.

The room had big sliding glass doors. On the inside, the room was circular, with half of the wall being the thick outer glass of the dome. Tobias even saw some fish swimming around outside. There were various gift shops selling novelties, and they passed the stand where you'd sign up for the tours. He knew someone who had gone on one of the tours. He'd said that it was terrific, and he had hoped to do it as well. If he wasn't barred after this, of course. They began walking towards their final destination, the airlock. They split up midway. Patrice veered left, walking towards a tour guide close to the airlock, already busy with a group. And he steered right. Tobias moved to the glass of the dome near the airlock. He rummaged around his cart and started spraying and wiping the glass, hoping he didn't look like a buffoon.

Patrice walked up to the tour guide; she straightened herself and took a deep breath. "Sir! Sir! Sir!" She said as she pushed past the group he was currently talking to. The group, which consisted of a pair of lovebirds, didn't push back. "Umm, yeah, umm, what is it?" The man said, well, boy, really. He was only a year or two older than her.

"I'm having a problem signing up," she said matter of factly, attempting to take control of the conversation. "Um yeah, I can't help," the tour guide said, trying to get her to go away. "Who would I talk to then?" She almost put her hands on her hips but decided that would be putting it on too thick. "Umm,

Tom over there can help you," he said, pointing to the man at the signup booth. "He's been no help at all; in fact, he's been quite rude to me!" She said. "Well, um, we'll go talk to him," he said and started walking, leaving behind the lovebirds, who looked very confused. As she began to walk away, she couldn't help but glance at Tobias, who was washing the same spot repeatedly. He looked like a buffoon.

Tobias was surprised that Patrice could be that mean, even more so when she began arguing with the man at the signup booth and the tour guide. He almost just stood there and watched but then remembered the plan. He moved his cart into the airlock. It was spacious for an airlock, and actually, not many people could see into the back of the airlock. There were racks of diving suits, five aside. A few of them were missing. With his heart thumping in his chest, he carefully unclipped one of the bulky suits and gently lowered it to the floor. He then gently kicked the cart three times, waited a moment, and then kicked it two more times. Elroy emerged from under the cloth covering the cart and grabbed the suit with his arms and legs. With the suit in a bear hug, Elroy rolled back onto the cart. He was surprised that one, Elroy was that strong, and two, that the suit even fit underneath the cart. "What are you doing!" A voice said behind him. His heart skipped a few beats as he turned around to see a security guard. He took a few mental deep breaths. "What'd you mean?! I'm cleaning!" he said. "Well, you can't be in the airlock while there are people out there," he said, gesturing to the empty suit racks. Tobias feigned an annoyed sigh and pulled his cart backward out of the airlock. "Hey, I've never seen you here before," said the guard. "Well, you better get used to it! I'm here to stay!" Tobias yelled over his shoulder as he pushed the cart toward the exit. "Where are you going then?" The security guard asked. "Lunch break," Tobias responded as he left the room. "Lunch? Already?" The guard mumbled to himself. When he left the aquarium, Tobias saw Patrice sitting against the wall near the doors. "There you are. I was worried you were caught," she said. "Same; I thought maybe you were arrested or something," Tobias said. "Arrested? No, I was just chewed out by the manager and barred for a month," she said. They walked in silence for a few blocks before she said, "You got it?" He nodded. They walked the rest of the way in silence, with the only sound being the small, plastic wheels of the cart against the sidewalk. When they got inside the workshop's storefront, Elroy rolled out from underneath the cart, suit in hands. "It's so heavy, and that cart is so uncomfortable," he said, out of breath. "So unless we're going to do that again, we've only got one suit," Patrice said as she helped Elroy to his feet. "Why would we need more than one?" Asked Tobias, "I can think of many reasons, one being if the submarine floods," Patrice said. "Well, if the submarine floods, we're dead anyway. It's not like we can walk back to the dome," Tobias said. "Stop freaking her out," said Elroy as he stretched his aching limbs. "So, who gets the suit?" Patrice said. "Definitely, Elroy. He's the only one who's used one before," Tobias said. "You have?" Patrice said. "Yeah, but it's nothing special, just some repairs on the outside of the dome, once," Elroy said. "Still, that's more than either of us," Patrice said.

Having stolen the two most essential items, they opted to acquire the rest legally.

Elroy bought the air filters. Nobody thought anything of his purchases, as almost all the air in the dome was recycled, and some people had their own recyclers and needed filters for them. Patrice and Tobias saved and bought canned, non-perishable food. It took almost two weeks, but they got everything they needed and stashed it at Elroy's house, where they were currently gathered. "I think that's everything," Tobias said. "Not so fast; we've got one more step," Elroy said. "Ugh, but that one sounds hard," Tobias said. "Don't worry, I'll be there, supervising," Patrice said. Later that day, they snuck back into the submarine pens and to the submarine they claimed. Patrice brought a folding chair, sat on the dock, and waved goodbye as Elroy lowered his welding mask, and the two of them descended into the submarine. She was surprised by how quiet it was; the only noise she could hear, besides the omnipresent creaking, came from the hatch. After a few minutes, she wished she'd brought something to read. Then she thought about how she should probably be at the pawnshop and that she was wasting her time. But even though she wasn't helping, it was nice to be present. She stared at the submarine, and sure it was big. But was it big enough to house the three of them for who knows how long? She didn't consider herself claustrophobic, but it seemed daunting. But if Elroy's father was really out there, she'd do just about anything to help him. Tobias sure would. And she expected that if one of her parents went missing, they'd risk life and limb to help her. Suddenly a figure appeared out the hatch. It was Elroy, his welding mask had disappeared, and he held a full trash bag in his hands. He climbed down the submarine and onto the dock. He rested the full trash bag near the cart, which held all their supplies. "Okay, we do actually need your help," He said, out of breath. "With what?" She asked. "It's so dirty, gross, and disgusting in there. We need you to help clean," He said. "I can smell it from here," she said, visibly disgusted. "If it's okay, I think I'll pass," she said. Elroy laughed as he grabbed an empty trash bag and headed back into the submarine. She'd risk a lot, but that sounded so gross.

The rest of the renovations took another few hours, during which she did go and fetch something to read and a reading light. After they were gone, they gave her a tour of the submarine. They led her down the hatch and into the submarine. The hatch led down into the bunk room. "There used to be four bunks, but we tore out this lower one and replaced it with this desk, where most of the equipment from the workshop will go, including the radio," Elroy said; Tobias nodded proudly. They moved forwards into the next room. "This is the pilot's room. To be honest, we didn't touch much in here in case we'd break something," Elroy said; Tobias nodded proudly. "Do either of you know what any of these buttons do?" Patrice said. "Well, no, but I did find this," Tobias said, holding up a book called the 'Pilot's Handbook' "So I think I'll be fine," He continued. They passed through the bunk room to get to the next room. There were three suit racks, one of which held their one and only suit. "We didn't know it when we first looked, but we've got a moon pool!" Elroy said, "Isn't that cool?" said Tobias. Patrice looked down and saw a pattern on the floor, "What's a moon pool?" she asked.

"So this bit of the floor opens to the water beneath. So that I could lower myself down in the diving suit," Elroy said. The next room was clearly the engine room; it also housed a lot of other machinery. "So this is the engine room, as well as the storage room," Elroy said, gesturing toward the several large shelves. "Are you sure it's a good idea to keep all our stuff in one place?" She asked. "I don't know, but each room, except the moon pool room, has storage in the floor," Said Elroy; Tobias nodded proudly.
"Nice, so I guess we start moving all our stuff here now?" Patrice asked. "Basically," said Elroy. They exited the submarine and walked down the dock,

pulling their cart with them. "For the rest of the day, though, I'd like to take a break," Elroy said; Tobias nodded in agreement.

Since Elroy would be the one in the diving suit and Tobias was going to attempt to pilot the submarine, Patrice decided to read up on radio operations in her downtime. She was reading when Elroy and Tobias entered the pawnshop. "What's up?" Tobias said. "Not much," she said. "We came over to see if you wanted to talk about a schedule?" Elroy said. "Sure, here?" She said. "I mean, no one else is here," Elroy said as he and Tobias sat down. "So, what is it you need to talk to me about?" She said. "Well, we wanted to know when you wanted to go," Tobias said. "Well, I think I'm about as ready as I can be," she said. "Well, we just finished moving all the supplies to the submarine," Elroy said. "We're ready to go as soon as possible," Tobias said. "We're doing all this for Elroy's dad, I'm sure that my parents will be happy to have me out of their hair, but we don't know about you," he continued. Patrice let out a heavy sign. "I'll be fine. How about in two days, on the weekend," she said. "Sounds good," Elroy said. Tobias nodded. They continued to talk for a little while, but she could tell that they'd said their piece.

And so they soon left. And when they did, Patrice reached under the counter and withdrew a crumpled piece of paper. She put it on the counter, smoothed it, and began writing a note.

Chapter 10

Shaun woke, and his heart immediately began thumping. He rolled over in his bed. Findings that his wife wasn't there made him worry further. He rolled back over and checked the clock. He signed with relief he wasn't late. He quickly got dressed and headed down the hallway to the kitchen/living room. He found his wife had already prepared breakfast, and his wife and daughter were already eating. He quickly sat down and began to eat his portion of eggs. "Good morning," his wife, Esmerelda, said. "Good morning," He replied, his mouth of full of eggs. After a few seconds of silence, "How's the job? Are you enjoying it?" He asked his daughter. "It's good, though it's not very busy," Patrice responded. "Y'know, I keep meaning to pop by the pawnshop," he said. "Yeah, it's a shame you're so busy," she said. "I know you're upset that I've increased my hours, but it's how we can live like this. Y'know me and your grandma lived in the slums before we came down here. Down here, engineers are at a premium," he finished with a chuckle. Patrice let out a sign. "I'm not upset, just sad," she said. "I know, but I'll still be here on the weekends," he said reassuringly. "Yes, but it's more than that," she said, picking at the remains of her eggs. "I know, I know," he said. His face lit up, "Well, tomorrow's the weekend; how about we do something!" He said excitedly. "Wouldn't that be great" his wife chimed in.

"Yeah, we could go to the park or the aquarium," he said. Patrice chuckled. "The park would be great," she said. He didn't know what she found funny about that but was happy to see her laugh. "The park it is then!" He said. "I'll pack lunches," Esmerelda said. "Right now, though, I've got to get going," he said. He quickly finished the remainder of his eggs and, with a wave, took off out the door.

Work was going fantastic. He had just come out of a meeting when they broke for lunch. He had a second wind hit him. And since they finished early, it would be a slightly longer lunch break. He decided to make good on his promises and headed down the winding staircases of the office to the ground floor and headed for their favorite restaurant. He bought two bags of food and headed for the pawnshop.

When he arrived he could see Patrice was with her friends, he liked them both, but sometimes Tobias could be a bad influence. They sat on old stools while she was still at the counter. He let himself in and was met with a great big smile from Patrice. She ran towards him and gave him a big hug. "You got food!" She said as she returned to the counter. "I did," he said as he set down the bags on the counter. "Though only enough for two," he said as he looked at her friends. "Don't worry about it; we've got to go get something to eat as well," Tobias said. "See you later," Elroy said; they left with a wave. They ate while chatting about nothing important. When they finished, he waved goodbye and returned to his work, reinvigorated.

When he left, Patrice was filled with guilt. She contemplated canceling but quickly decided against it; she would go. But she still felt terrible about it.

The next day, while Elroy and Tobias prepared, Patrice was in the park laughing and playing. Patrice and her dad arrived early and stayed there all day. Towards the end of the day, when the lights were dimming, the park sky was a shade of orange as the large overhead light tried to simulate a sunset. "Y'know, it's hard to believe that you'll never see a sunset," he said. They were lying on their large picnic blanket. Esmeralda had left not long ago to go home and start dinner. "I don't know what all the fuss is about, I've seen pictures, and sure it looks nice, but.." she let the sentence trail off. "Pictures don't do it justice. The vast sky goes all orange and purple, and the sun... I don't know how to explain it," he said, full of nostalgia. A few moments of silence. "Do you ever think we'll reclaim the surface?" She asked. "I don't know. Probably, but not in my lifetime," he said. "But we can't reclaim anything in our current state," he continued.

"What do you mean by that?" She asked. "Everything. But most importantly, the domes would need to be reconnected," he said. "Not to get all scary, but if we continue like this, it's only a matter of time before we all starve," he said. "Oh," she said.

"Yeah, but I hear they're working on it. But I just hope they do it in time," he said. "Why can't we reconnect with the other domes now? What's stopping us?" Patrice asked. "Well, we used to communicate and send goods back and forth with a network of pneumatic tubes. But they were all destroyed at around the same time; nobody knows what happened. Some claim sabotage, but we've no evidence of that. After the lines were cut, we sent submarines back and forth. That worked for a little while until they started disappearing. A third of the submarines sent out would never return. We couldn't figure out why and we couldn't sustain the losses. All the other domes had the same problem." "That's weird and spooky," Patrice said. "Yeah, I know, and I know you're eager for us to reclaim the surface. It would solve a lot of our problems, but it's hard to properly convey the scale and magnitude of the war that preceded the flood. Entire continents were wiped clean in days. Let me correct that; I shouldn't say clean; they were anything but clean. Filled with radioactive, well, everything and ruins. There isn't much to reclaim. Though Africa probably still has some arable land," he said. "I know, but it sounds so cool to explore something new," she said. "I know. I've had the worst cabin fever for the last two decades," he said. "That's enough scary talk. Let's catch up with your mother," he said. They packed up and headed back home. Esmeralda met them with food, and they went to sleep full and exhausted.

He awoke and, for a moment, panicked when he looked at his clock but calmed when he realized it was still the weekend. He turned and saw Esmarelda was still asleep. He got out of bed as quietly as possible and entered the hallway. Patrice's door was ajar; he peeked in and didn't see her. He figured she must already be up. He went into with kitchen/living room with a "Good morning!" But his heart sank a little bit when she wasn't there. But he calmed when he saw a note on the counter. She probably went to hang out with her friends on the weekend. He had hoped to spend another day with her, but he understood. This got him thinking about his friends. He hadn't spoken to Jim in a while. Maybe while Patrice spent the weekend with her friends, he should spend his weekend with his friends. He pondered this as he picked up the note and began to read. His stomach sank lower and lower the longer he read.

Dear Dad or Mom,

You may have noticed that I've left and packed a few of my things. I'm going to be spending a few days with my friends. I might be gone for longer, though, as I don't know exactly how long I'll be gone. I might be back as early as this time next week, though don't count on it. I promise I'll be safe, don't worry about me. I'm sorry to break it to you like this, but I couldn't tell you this to your face. Plus, you'd try to stop me.

PS. I'm not doing anything weird, I promise.

Patrice had tears in her eyes as she clambered aboard the submarine. Elroy and Tobias didn't feel the same. She understood why Elroy didn't feel like she did; the whole point of this was to find his dad. But she couldn't comprehend why Tobias was okay, eager even, to leave his parents. Patrice had met Tobias' parents only once. But they seemed like friendly, caring people.

She wasn't the last down the hatch. Elroy entered after her and sealed it behind them. As soon as he entered, Tobias went into the pilot's room. She was skeptical that he could do it, but she supposed they had no other options. That left Elroy and Patrice sitting in the bunk room. She expected the submarine to go forward; she really did. But she somehow wasn't surprised when she heard, "Umm, guys?" From the front of the submarine. "Yeah?" Elroy said, "how do we get the pen door open?" Tobias said. "There should be a button, right?" Said Elroy as he squeezed into the cockpit beside Tobias.

After much fussing and arguing, they determined that there, in fact, wasn't a button. She heard something about a manual switch, and Elroy was undoing the hatch, "Come on, I need your help," he said to Patrice. They both exited the hatch and walked along the dock to the edge of the dome. There was a large metal wheel. Elroy tried it, and it didn't move. With her help, they managed to move it just the slightest amount. As soon as they did, they heard a rumbling from deep within. The wheel became significantly easier to move. As they moved it, the pen door opened. As the door opened, a large wave of water swept the submarine. They realized then that the pen that their submarine was in wasn't quite full of water. It was now, though, the submarine sat much higher, the wave swept across the dock, just enough to get their shoes wet. They clambered back aboard, Elroy sealed the hatch, and this time, they moved.

The atmosphere was one of stress. They were all worried about something. Tobias about not crashing the submarine, Elroy about finding his dad, and Patrice about the tight spaces. She had convinced herself that she'd be fine, but she wasn't. It felt like she could feel the weight of all the water above them, and she swore the submarine was shrinking. To distract herself from this, she began studying their route. She sat down at the desk with which they'd replaced the fourth bunk. On the desk were all the documents from the workshop. Some were piled on the desk, while the more important stuff was pinned to the wall. Next to all the paper was the radio. They hadn't used it except to test that it worked. She examined the paper that dictated their first destination. "What're you doing?" Said Elroy, clearly bored. He was the designated diver and, as such, was currently unoccupied. "Just double-checking our route," she said. "Well, if you find anything new, let me know," he said from his seat on the bunk opposite the desk. After laying out the route in her mind and comparing coordinates to maps, she felt an excitement emanating deep from within her chest. She was just like the explorers of old! She just wished she was deciphering a treasure map, and then her dreams would be complete. While she had a great time, one can only double-check maps so many times. Elroy was likewise bored, though Tobias was anything but bored. They hadn't considered the inherent boredom in traveling through vast swaths of the sea at a snail's pace. All they brought along for entertainment was chess and checkers, but no one really knew how to play chess, so Patrice and Elroy played checkers for hours.

When Tobias called out to them, they were stacking their checkers to try to make the tallest tower. "Hey, I think we're here," said Tobias. When they didn't hurry, "You're really gonna want to see this," he said. Excitedly, they all three squeezed into the cockpit. Patrice hadn't been in the cockpit before; she expected a big window; instead, almost every inch was covered with instruments. "See what?" She said. "This," Tobias said, pointing at the sonar. She was about to say something, but Tobias cut her off. "Give me a second," Tobias said. He reached for his book and opened a page he had bookmarked. He studied the book for a few seconds and then scanned the instruments. Finally, he found what he was looking for and pressed a button, and one of the panels lit up with grainy camera footage. "That," Tobias said. The camera showed what seemed to be an old sunken ship. Patrice thought it was a destroyer because of its size. It was gray and red. And very obviously went down in combat, as there were several large holes in the side. And they could only see one side as it sat at a steep angle.

"So let me get this straight," Elroy said. "There's a distress signal coming from this old, sunken navy vessel?" He continued. Tobias shook his head. "Actually, no, there's not." "Why'd you think that is?" Elroy asked. "I suppose if your dad had already been here, he'd have turned it off," Patrice said. Elroy's dad had left them the coordinates for where he planned to go. He also said that he was going to each of these sites because he heard distress signals and wanted to help. "Now?" Elroy said. Tobias nodded.

Chapter 11

The suit was old and worn, clearly having had a long life. Elroy had only put on a suit once, and he had the help of an instructor and specialist; even then, it took a while. This time he had to go with what he could remember. It took him a long time to get suited. He really didn't want to rush it. The big, bulky, bronze diving suit gave him very little mobility. Tobias had opened the moon pool, and the two of them were now watching him try and get down it. He could have just jumped, but that scared him considerably. Instead, he tried to sit with his legs in the pool and then slide in. He got as far as bending over, and then he fell headfirst into the water. He was disoriented and frightened. But it seemed he had remembered well, as no water was leaking in. They weren't parked very far from the seafloor. And so he didn't fall very far before he landed with a thump face first on the bottom of the ocean. As Elroy unsteadily righted himself, Patrice rushed to the radio, through which she could communicate to him. "Are you okay?" Patrice's voice came through the radio in his helmet. He could barely even tell it was her, but he could hear the words fine enough. "Yeah, just had a bit of a fall," he said. He had his own oxygen, but he was breathing through a line attached to the submarine for the most part. He untangled this line from his legs and stood. He took a few wobbly steps and saw just how far the wreck was. It was going to take a while. Soon though, he got the hang of walking underwater. The suit was very heavy, and he doubted he could move it under his own power. Instead, it had several pistons and the like to help him. It did take him a while, but he was surprised by how quickly he got there. He was also surprised by just how long the line was. The ship looked much more wrecked up close. "Umm, how am I supposed to get in?" He said after surveying the side of the ship. "Tobias says to climb the side and enter through the lowest hole," Patrice said. He took a few steps back, sprinted towards the ship, and jumped. He wasn't actually going that fast, and because of the weight of the suit, he didn't jump very high either. He hit the ship and slid back down for lack of handholds. He could hear the screech of metal on metal when he slid. He was about to attempt the same thing again. But before he started his run, he saw several large pieces of metal stacked in such a way that he reckoned he could climb them. He approached and examined them. They looked recent, at least compared to the wreck. He found that they were even easier to climb than he had anticipated, and soon he climbed the side and entered the ship. He fell a few feet onto the opposite wall. The room was dark. He turned on his headlamp. It lit up the room, but he still couldn't tell what the room's original purpose was pre-wreck. "Tobias wants me to ask you what those were that you climbed on," Patrice said. "Tell him I don't know," he said. He examined the floor, which was actually the wall. And saw scratch marks. He would have concluded that they were just damaged had they not led up the wall, which was originally the floor, and through an open door. He scuttled up and through the door. He was perched on the door frame, examining the room. It seemed to be some kind of storage room. What was strange was that all the lockers were flung open. He supposed it was possible, though unlikely, that the crew of a sinking ship would run far below deck to rummage through supplies. He thought it was much more likely that someone had looted the ship after it sank. He gave the lockers a quick once over. He didn't really know what he was looking for, but the lockers were almost completely empty. He climbed the lockers and lept from the doorway to the stairwell. As he climbed the stairs, he came across many rooms that he had no clue as to their function. Eventually, he reached the top deck. He ran up the stairs and nearly fell off the deck and off the ship. He managed to catch himself. He considered trying to scale the deck but quickly decided against it. He ducked back into the stairs and moved horizontally until he reached his destination, the bridge. It was filled with instruments but, unlike the submarine, had huge windows. One of the consoles was blinking. He briefly wondered what was powering it while moving toward it. As he got closer, he could hear something; he couldn't make out the words through the water and the metal suit. The screen, though, seemed to have a transcript scrolling across it. It read, 'SOS we've been struck by an enemy vessel and are rapidly taking on water. If there are any nearby vessels, we'd greatly appreciate some help'. It scrolled across the screen, repeating. "Hey, I think I've found your distress signal, though it must not be broadcasting anymore," he said. "Any sign of life?" Patrice asked. "Nothing conclusive. I'll talk more about it once I'm back aboard," he said. "Roger," she replied. After a short break, he began the tedious task of following his line back through the winding hallways and back to the submarine.

Once he was underneath the submarine, they

reopened the moon pool. He then had to scale his line up to the submarine. It was challenging, and it ended with him exhausted. Though it took maybe ten minutes to get him out of the suit. Once he was out, he flopped onto the bottom bunk. "Who knew away missions were so tedious," Tobias said. "Who knew they were so exhausting," said Elroy. Tobias sat on the end of his bed above Elroy, and Patrice sat on the chair next to the desk, facing him. "So, tell us about those non-conclusive signs of life," she said. "Well, it was clear that everybody originally on the ship, well they didn't farewell. But there were a few signs of more recent activity. For example, with the metal piled against the side of the ship, I think someone struggled to climb up. Second, the lockers were opened and ransacked not too long ago," Elroy said. "Hmm," Tobias said. They pondered over this for a while until it was time for dinner, something they'd all been dreading. There hadn't been a galley on the submarine, and they hadn't added one. While they were handy with a welder and hammer, neither of them were electricians. So all they had to eat was cold canned food. They all shared an extra-large can of chili. They then all settled into their bunks and tried to sleep.

Chapter 12

The next day they quickly got moving while Patrice and Elroy attempted to play chess. After losing, Elroy sat back "Y'know, we've not actually decided on a name for the submarine yet," he said. "Yeah, I've been thinking about that, but I can't think of anything good," Tobias chimed in. "Hmm, how about the USS Mayflower?" Patrice said.

Elroy chuckled "Wow, you really think highly of our journey," he said. "What's the Mayflower?" Said Tobias, appearing next to them. "What are you doing here?!" said Patrice "Yeah, who's piloting the submarine?" Elroy said. "Relax, it basically pilots itself, and plus, I couldn't miss out on naming the submarine," he said.

"How about the USS Invulnerable," Elroy said. "No, that's just inviting trouble," Tobias said. "Instead, how about the Destroyer," Tobias said. "But this submarine doesn't have any guns," Patrice said. "How about the Flying Fish," Elroy suggested. "Sounds a bit silly," Patrice said. "Yeah, we need to strike fear in the hearts of our enemies," Tobias said. "I standby the Mayflower plus, I don't see you guys coming with anything better," Patrice said. Elroy chuckled "No, no, that's fine. The Mayflower it is then!" He declared. "You're going to have to explain that to me sometime," Tobias mumbled as he returned to the cockpit. They reset the chess board, and time dragged on. "There's no way the bishop can do that!" Said Elroy after losing again. Patrice began her rebuttal, but Tobias cut her off "We're approaching the next site," he said. They all once again crammed themselves into the cockpit. "We should really get some windows in here," Patrice said as Tobias gestured to a point on the map. "Unlike the last one, though, there's barely anything here," he said, pointing to the sonar. As they neared closer, Tobias flipped on the camera. It showed an abandoned diving suit sat in a crater. Elroy shivered. "I'm still not receiving a signal," said Patrice "Well, it's marked on the map," Tobias said. He slapped Elroy on the back "Good luck," he said. It was much less frustrating suiting up the second time, though it still took an annoying amount of time. Eventually, though, he was floating down the moon pool, gracefully compared to his previous attempt. He began waddling, and within only a few moments, he was only a few yards from the suit. He paused, took a few deep breaths. He was scared that whatever happened to that suit would also happen to his. He stepped into the crater, and when he didn't immediately explode, he felt safe to continue to the suit. As he got closer, it became clearer that the suit was heavily damaged. He could see several large dents and maybe even a hole from here. He moved closer. Eventually, he was at arm's length. He reached for the helmet and removed the faceplate. He was relieved that it was empty. "Anybody in there?" Patrice asked. "No," he responded. "Any sign as to how it ended up like that?" she said. "Not yet," he said. He searched around the suit, and it wasn't long before he found what he was looking for. Right where the suit met the helmet was a serial number. He studied it for a few seconds "This suit wasn't built in Dome Eight," he said. "Woah," Patrice said in awe. "I think I've found a clue," he said. He saw tracks. There was an intermittent trail that looked like the suit had been dragged. There were two other tracks on either side of it; they were footprints. These tracks weren't new; they were prints made in soft rock, the kind of material that only a heavy suit would leave tracks in. "I've found some tracks. I'm going to follow them," he said. "Okay, be careful," Patrice said. "Will do," he said as he set off.

The tracks led behind a rock formation, and so he was quickly out of sight of the Mayflower. After a few hundred feet, the tracks stopped at the mouth of a cave.He flipped on his headlamp and continued in. The cave wasn't the deepest, and after a dozen strides, he found where the tracks originated. It seemed to be some kind of camp, with watertight crates stacked in the corners and oxygen canisters everywhere. He found a notebook on one of these crates. It was wrapped in a plastic seal to protect it from the water. He opened a hatch on his suit, revealing a small storage compartment. He put the sealed notebook inside, then clamped it shut. "I've found something interesting," he said, but he got no reply. He reasoned the cave walls were too thick for his weak radio to penetrate. He waddled back out the cave and back along the tracks until he was in sight of the Mayflower again. When he reached the crater, he said, "Guys, I've found-" he stopped talking when he saw movement out of the corner of his vision. He whipped his head around as fast as the bulky suit and the surrounding water allowed. When he turned, he saw a long black shape staring at him. "Are you okay?" Patrice said, worried. "Umm, for the moment. But a tiger eel is currently staring me down," he said.

Tiger eels emerged during the War and subsequent Flood. They were long and black with brown stripes, and they were known for their suit busting capability. He had only heard of them the first time he was put into a diving suit. One would struggle to breach his suit, but it's not like he could stop it. It floated menacingly at eye level. He moved slowly backward, but for every inch he moved backward, the eel moved forwards. The Mayflower began to drift towards him. "Tobias has a plan that might work. Get to the flat bit of rock to your left," Patrice said. He wordlessly complied, slowly turning and continuing to back away from the eel. But the large nine-foot eel was occasionally moving two inches when he moved one. Eventually, he reached the flat area that Patrice mentioned. The eel was just a stone's throw away. The Mayflower was now directly above him. The submarine then began to float downwards. He was scared of the eel, but now he was worried about being crushed. Elroy held his hands up as the eel got even closer, he doubted he could bat it away, but he was going to have to try. The Mayflower was now getting closer by the second. Suddenly he understood the plan, "Forward! Forward!" He shouted. The submarine lurched forward as the moon pool opened.

It was now just a few feet above him. He assumed that the eel, upon seeing the incoming crushing, would flee. He underestimated their ferocity when it instead charged at him. The Mayflower hit the seafloor with a noisy thud. Suddenly he was in the submarine, dripping wet, and the eel crushed. Patrice was standing next to the moon pool. He stepped onto the submarine as the moon pool closed. Patrice quickly helped him take off the helmet, and they were working on the rest of the suit when Tobias rushed in "Was that not the coolest thing I've ever done!" He said, pumping his fist in the air. Elroy chuckled "Yeah, saved my life, but you might want to get us off the seafloor," Elroy said as the moon pool closed. "Oh yeah," he said, running back. "I had no idea how big those things were," said Patrice. "Yeah, they're absolutely massive," he said. Once he was out of the suit, he reached into the compartment and withdrew the notebook "And look what I found," he said. "What does it say?" Patrice asked "Let's find out," he said. They were all sitting around the desk when Elroy broke the seal on the plastic. It was a pretty standard notebook, one that you could buy at any store. Written on the front of the notebook was *expedition log*. They huddled around Elroy as he opened the book. He read aloud, "day 38, our sub has just run aground. Thankfully everyone was able to get a suit in time. We've salvaged as much as we could, namely the oxygen canisters. I've decided to start this log in case something happens to us. Or rather. If something *doesn't* happen. Day 39, We've moved into a cave to hide from the population of tiger eels. They seem more aggressive than normal. It seems as if they're hellbent on tasting our blood. It seems I underestimated the difficulty of writing this. I've been writing with my hands against my chest, fitting both the pen and book inside my suit with me," Elroy paused. He skipped over a few days of little interest before continuing, "Day 43, The tiger eels have gotten even more aggressive, if that's even possible. They've started probing into our cave. We've managed to scare them off, but I doubt that's going to last much longer. In much lighter news, we have rescuers. Or at least a hope we do. We picked up a signal acknowledging our distress signal. They said they could save us, but only if we were able to reach some coordinates. The only problem? The tiger eels would rip us to shreds if we tried to make a break for it. So we've come up with a plan. We're going to go to our wreck and retrieve one of the inoperable spare suits if we can keep the eels at bay for that short trip. We'll then drag the spare suit into a large, open area. Then we'll turn on the beacon and run. Hopefully, the eels will be busy with it. We'll be leaving swiftly thereafter. So I'll have to abandon this book. I suppose I could carry it with me, but I'd like to leave it behind to explain what happened here if anyone ever stumbles upon our little failed expedition.

If you're reading this and you see five bodies lying on the bottom of the ocean, then you know what happened. But if you don't and would like to check up on us, written below are the coordinates that we received. Goodbye," After Elroy finished talking, the group fell silent. Patrice poked her head over Elroy's shoulder and took a good, long look at the coordinates. "Well, it's on the way to our next stop, might as well," she said. "I'm up for it," Tobias said. "Yeah, I'd like to go," said Elroy. "Well, let's get going then!" Said Tobias, eagerly entering the cockpit. They felt the lurch as the Mayflower set off.

Chapter 13

It took them a while to get to the coordinates the book specified. Elroy wondered how long it took the group since they had to walk the whole way. "What do you think we'll find there?" Elroy asked as he checked her king; he was getting better at chess. "I don't know, probably nothing," she said as she eliminated his piece that was checking her king. "Yeah, but I hope we find out what happened to them," he said. "I hope they're okay," she said. "Definitely," he said. After a few more games of chess and then an angry game of checkers, they arrived at their destination. Once again, they all huddled around Tobias' chair as they squinted at the camera. "Are you sure this is it?" Said Elroy. The low resolution on the camera made it impossible to see anything but the big picture, and the big picture was that there was nothing there. "Yes, and the sonar is showing nothing either," Tobias said. Elroy let out a breathy sigh. "I guess it's up to me then," he said. Not too long after that, he was in the deep blue. "I hope they're okay," Patrice said. "Yeah, it's all terrifying," he said. Eventually, he reached the center of the Mayflower's view. "Yeah, umm, I don't see anything. What now?" He said. "I don't know; look for clues or something," she said. "Thanks, very helpful," he said as he began surveying his surroundings. For what, he wasn't exactly sure. Eventually, he gave up walking around the area and sat down. Only then did he see the soft markings in the sand. It was faint, but the more he focused, the more he saw. He saw footprints walking towards a faint oval mark in the sand. He was no tracker but guessed this is where they went. "I've found some tracks in the sand," he said. "What kind of tracks?" Patrice asked. "Footprints, and it looks like a submarine touched down here," he said. "Hmm, so I guess they made this far," she said. "And it looks like they were picked up. The footprints go up to the oval and then disappear," he said. A few seconds passed while Elroy spun around, looking for further clues. "How do we tell where they went?" He asked. "How am I supposed to know? You're the one down there," she said. A few more seconds passed, nothing. Elroy paced back and forth, hoping to find something. He had almost given up when he saw a glint in the sand. He knelt in the sand and found the glint was coming from a metal nut. "Hey, I found some kind of nut," Elroy said. "Anything else?" Patrice asked. Elroy was about to say no, but he spotted something on a rock a few feet from where he found the nut. He picked up the nut and moved closer to examine the rock. It looked like some paint from the mystery submarine had been scraped off against the rock. "I found some paint on this rock," he said, gesturing exaggeratedly so that they could see it on the Mayflower's camera. "Anything special about the paint?" Patrice asked. "Doesn't look like it," He responded. "Okay, come back. I want to look at that thing you picked up," Patrice said. Elroy walked back to the Mayflower and clumsily entered.

Once inside, he handed the nut to Patrice, and she helped him unscrew his helmet. Tobias joined them in examining it. "It just looks like any other metal thingy," Patrice said, holding it up to her face. "Let me see," Elroy said. Patrice held it up so he could see it since his bulky metal hands were too big to properly handle it. "No, I do recognize it, but I don't remember where from," Elroy said. "Give it to me," Tobias said. He examined for a while, the answer on the tip of his tongue. "I remember learning about this. This is a nut that is only on submarines built after the flood. We came up with this bad boy all on our own," Tobias said. "Oh, now I remember!"

Elroy said. Elroy and Tobias launched into a conversation about how it was built and what niche it filled. Patrice interrupted halfway through by grabbing it from Tobias. "Guys, if it was only built after the flood, in our dome, then do you know what that means?" She said, bringing their previous conversation to a halt. They looked at each other, then at her.

"If you gave me enough time, I'd probably figure it out, but it'd be quicker if you just told us," Tobias said, shrugging. "That means that this submarine was from our dome," Patrice said. Elroy and Tobias both looked surprised. "Does that mean it's...?" Tobias said. "I hope so," Elroy said.

"Where was the paint that you saw?" Patrice asked. "I'll show you as soon as I've got this suit off," Elroy said. With Patrice and Tobias' help, it went much quicker than previously. Once he was out of his suit, they all squeezed into the cockpit, and he pointed to one of the rocks on the camera. "That probably means that the submarine went that way, right?" Patrice suggested. "Yeah, probably," Elroy said. "And it also probably means that it was piloted by an amateur. I know I've probably left quite a few paint marks behind us," Tobias said. "Since the markings were in the sand, does that mean it could still be nearby?" Patrice asked. "I dunno, the markings looked kinda old," Elroy said. "I could do an extra powerful sonar sweep, see if anything's nearby," Tobias said. Elroy shrugged. "Why not," he said.

Tobias got to work flipping switches and spinning dials and frequently referencing the handbook. Eventually, they heard a deep rumbling from the Mayflower as the engine tried to provide the power needed. It seemed to work as the sonar seemed to be revealing significantly more than before. After a good few minutes, nothing showed up. Tobias was about to shut it down when it picked something up. It was big, the size of a submarine. They cheered, and it got closer and closer. And as it got closer, they could get a picture of what it was. They didn't know what it was, but it wasn't a submarine, and it wasn't slowing down. Tobias quickly started up the Mayflower and began quickly going in the opposite direction. "What is that thing?!" Patrice said. "I don't know," Tobias said, his voice shaky. Patrice left the cockpit, trying not to panic.

While, unfortunately, the Mayflower was unarmed, it was fast. Initially built as a messenger submarine. Its job was to deliver messages between domes when the pneumatic lines were cut. As they reached their top speed, the threat lessened. However, it would still catch up with them, at least at its current speed, so they gathered to figure out a plan. "Maybe it'll tire itself out?" Elroy said. "That's assuming it's alive," Tobias pointed out; Patrice shuddered. "Okay. Let's say it's a submarine. Why would it be chasing us?" Elroy asked. "I dunno, pirates?" Tobias said. A significant vibration shook the Mayflower, nearly knocking the three of them over. Tobias rushed back to the cockpit, and the others followed.

"What the hell was that?!" Patrice shouted. "I don't know," Tobias said, busy with his instruments. Elroy saw that the shape on the sonar was getting much closer. The relatively flat seafloor gave way to a sizeable marine trench ahead of them. As they moved over it, Tobias looked back at them and then dove downwards into the trench. It was wide, more than enough to fit both them and their pursuer. "What's your plan?" Patrice asked. "I don't have one, but I figured that being down here was better than being up there," Tobias said. As they continued along the trench, their pursuer was catching up. Another significant vibration shook them, and Elroy couldn't help but liken it to a roar this time. Tobias turned on the rear camera, which had been empty. Now reaching out from the murky water were at least a dozen tentacles, sometimes getting way too close. "That's hands down the worst thing I've ever seen," Patrice said with a strange calm. Elroy, on the other hand, was panicking quite badly. "What about down there?" Patrice said, ignoring Elroy's hyperventilating. What Patrice pointed at on the camera was a small hole in the side of the trench. It didn't look like they could fit through. "I mean, I guess it's either that or..." Tobias didn't finish the sentence. Instead, he steered the Mayflower toward the opening.

Chapter 14

Tobias' heart nearly stopped when the Mayflower did. Slowly though, the Mayflower squeezed its way into the opening. The sides of the Mayflower scraping against the rock made him cringe. He saw one of the tentacles touch the submarine on the rear camera. It seemed confused as to why its prey had stopped moving. Another probing tentacle reached right for the propeller. The tip of the tentacle was severed when it made contact with the rapidly spinning blades. Another roar shook the Mayflower, much larger than the previous two. After the roar subsided, two dozen tentacles reached out for the Mayflower. But the Mayflower had made it through the tightest of the cave, and as it began to widen, the Mayflower was able to quickly dart into the small cave. The cave turned out to be a dead-end, but they were able to stay just out of reach of the grasping tentacles. Tobias began to power off some systems, and they spent the rest of the day and the subsequent night in the cave.

None of them slept particularly well.

The next day they tentatively squeezed out of

the cave. Then, with the monster nowhere to be seen, they exited the trench and headed to their next destination. "No wonder all the submarines started disappearing," Tobias muttered.

They traveled for a little while before arriving at their destination. They were amazed when they first saw it. It seemed like some destroyed buildings. It looked like it was once a series of small buildings with a large one at the center. Most of the buildings were in some state of ruin and decay, but the large one seemed like it might still be watertight. This time it was Patrice who slapped his back. "Good luck," she said.

Once again, he suited up, it was getting faster, but it was still annoying. Because of his encounter with the tiger eel, he had a dive knife strapped to the outside of the suit.

Once he got to the first ruin, he took his time to examine it. It was a small-ish building made out of metal. It was so destroyed that it looked like somebody had crumpled it and thrown it away like paper. He couldn't deduce anything related to its function. He moved to the next building. This one was smaller and seemed to be some kind of small warehouse, but it too was significantly destroyed. The next building's roof hadn't yet completely collapsed. And as he moved through the small building, he hit something with his foot. Examining further, he found a trapdoor. "Hey, I've found a hatch in this one," he said, waving to the Mayflower, floating ominously overhead. "Creepy, what's in it?" Patrice said. "I haven't checked; give me a second," he said as he began pulling on the trapdoor. It took a little while to unstick the door, but eventually, it gave way. Revealing a flooded rocky tunnel, "Huh, it's some kind of tunnel," he said. "Hmm, that makes sense. I wouldn't want to have to suit up every time you wanted to go between buildings," she said. He left the trapdoor open, but he really didn't want to go down there. The next building was the big one. He expected there to be a door on the outside, but he was still surprised when he found one. "Hey, there's a door on this building," he said. It looked like some kind of airlock. "Can you go through it?" Patrice asked. "I'll try," Elroy responded. There wasn't any power, so he had to use the crank on the door to get it to open. After much time and effort, he got the outer door open. He entered the airlock and went to try the crank on the inner door. But it immediately caught on something and wouldn't do anything. "The outer door opened, but the inner door seems stuck on something," Elroy said. "Well, I guess that means you're going down the tunnel," she said. He sighed and made his way to the open trapdoor. He stood over it, his heart racing. "Okay, well, I'm probably going to lose contact," he said. "Understood," she replied. And with that, he climbed down.

It was tight and dark. Unfortunately, in order to fit down the tunnel, he had to disconnect his line. He still had an hour or two of air, but he didn't want to be down here longer than he had to. His head made a horrible noise as it scraped along the roof, but he was already crouched and couldn't go much lower without crawling. It was so narrow that his sides scraped against the walls. His bulky suit didn't help, but he would've struggled even without it. He flicked on his headlight. He was relieved when he could see the end of the tunnel. But it still took him over a dozen minutes to cross the relatively short tunnel. Once he got to the end of the tunnel, his head stopped scraping against the rough stone. He looked up and saw another trapdoor. This one was much easier to open, though, as all he needed to do was stand up. The first thing he noticed was how nice it was to stand upright again. His head was at floor level, and he couldn't see much as the room was pitch black. He climbed out of the tunnel with incredible difficulty. It was already hard to climb underwater, but out of the water, it was near impossible with the weight of the suit. Eventually, though, he managed. After sweeping the room with his light, he gathered that this was a room for suiting up, not dissimilar to the room on the Mayflower. He noticed the other side of the airlock, though it was covered with debris. The room was small and only had two doors. The airlock and an interior door. He approached this door. He was about to open it when a paranoid part of his brain started worrying. He grabbed his knife; he wasn't sure what he was afraid of or what he would use the knife against, but a combination of the dark and being alone really put him on edge. Though the thick metal suit did make him feel a good bit safer. He opened the door, revealing another dark room. As he crept through, the creaking and groaning of the building made him even more paranoid. This room seemed to be a living space with furniture dispersed around the room. The only door out of that room led to a T intersection. On a whim, he went right. This room seemed to be important. He found lots of maps and plans on desks. He glanced around the room and decided to explore the other room and then come back. He exited back into the T and went the other way. This room was dominated by a large, dormant generator. The only other thing of note in the room was a large radio setup. For all he knew about machines, he knew little about radios. But he bet this one was powerful; at least it looked the part. Upon further investigation of the radio, he found the on switch had been torn off. He still reckoned he could get it working. But a note was attached near the broken switch.

DO NOT USE it read in big, hastily scribbled letters. Elroy hurried back to the other room for answers. A stack of papers was on one of the desks, all stapled together. The topmost paper had IMPORTANT written on it, so he went there first. He picked up the papers and flipped to the following paper, which was tricky because of his reduced dexterity from the big, metal gloves. He began reading.

Okay, so I know this is a long shot, but what have these past couple of weeks been if not a long shot. We're abandoning this place for reasons I'll get to later, and I figured if anyone in the future stumbles across this place, they might want to know what happened. And I'm here to provide. And so, even though my writing will probably be lost when the building collapses and is lost to time, I'm hoping otherwise. Or, even if it is lost, I feel good to get this off my chest. Okay, from now on, I'm going to assume someone has found this and that you're from the future, okay? So, there's one crucial thing you need to know. The radio? It attracts them, do not use it. If you look around the room, assuming it is still intact, you'll find drawings of them, artists' interpretations, really. As they're near impossible to see, despite their size. You may know them as something else, but we've always called them Krakens. We don't know where the term came from. But since the flood, many years ago, they've been nothing but a myth, a bedtime story. And, despite my academic tendencies, I wish they'd remained undiscovered. So, in short, the radio attracts them. And, I cannot reiterate this enough, DO NOT USE IT.

Another thing, if you've looked around this room, again assuming it's intact, you've probably found some maps. If the room isn't intact, I'll say it here. I spent most of my life in dome one. If you are also from dome one, then welcome, brother. I'm sure *you already know about this project, and hey, if I survived and made it home, bring this back to me, yeah? But we've heard of another seven domes. Apparently, all eight domes were supposed to be interconnected. And only a few days underwater, and all the connections were severed. At the time, we thought it was a series of natural phenomena coincidentally happening near the same time. But thanks to our work here, we've discovered it was almost certainly the Krakens. Now assuming you aren't from dome one, as this project was pretty big news, then let me explain this little project. So, dome one, as you may or may not know, was the military and command dome. Now, when we lost connection, we lost connection with the most vital dome, dome two. They made all the food, and you don't stand much of a chance without food. We lived off emergency rations when we first came down here, but that only lasted so long. Now, we mostly rely on hunting. We'll use our extensive military vessels for hunting some of the larger sea beasts. But that's about to run out. As the big military stuff is starting to break down. This stuff was built to last, but it's been decades, and the cherry on top is we're almost out of fuel. So, as it stands, we're not doing great. So, we built this shack. It was meant to project a powerful radio signal in hopes of establishing a connection with another dome. Any dome would have been fine, but dome two, with its food production, or dome eight, with their maintenance and fuel synthesis capabilities. But, as you've noticed, that didn't go well. So, after many close calls with the Krakens and one not-so-close call, we're packing up, never to come back. And hey, if you are from a different dome, I'll love to meet you. Look for Professor Bentley. I work at the campus, can't miss it. And, again, assuming the rest of our work isn't intact, here are my coordinates.*

Elroy finished reading. Slack-jawed, he stood there for a while. Eventually, he recovered. He quickly searched through all the rooms he had been through, paranoia replaced by excitement. Finally, he found a sizeable watertight bag, which he stuffed as many documents into as possible, as well as the stack of papers. He was sad about how much he had to leave behind, but he was running a tad low on oxygen, and as exciting as this was, he was not going through that tunnel more than he had to. So, he tried the airlock. But he felt stupid once he remembered that the airlock had no power. And so, he resigned himself to going through the tunnel.

It was as bad as he remembered it, but after much cramping, he poked his head out of the trapdoor, "Elroy, are you there?" "Yes! And you're never going to believe what I found! And also turn off the radio," he said as he shuffled toward the Mayflower.

Once he had taken off the suit, he tossed the still damp bag onto the bed. "This is all stuff from dome one," he said. "You're kidding," Tobias said. Patrice unzipped the bag and started rummaging through it. "Nope," he said. "Wow," Patrice said as she held up one of the maps. "Now, I've not read any of these, except that one," he said, pointing to the stack of papers. While Patrice looked through maps, Tobias picked up the stack of papers. He quickly skimmed it, but his eyes bulged when he saw the coordinates at the end. "Um, so this is all well and good. But I've got some bad news," Tobias said. "What?" Patrice said. "Well, if we go to these coordinates, we won't have enough food to make it back," he said. Silence followed. "Oh," said Elroy. "Well, if we get there, they must have food, right?" Patrice said, "Well, they said they were experiencing a food shortage," Elroy said, gesturing to the stack of papers.

"I say we push on," Patrice said. "I don't know,'" said Tobias. "Really? I thought you'd be up for it?" She said. "Yeah, well, this time, the stakes are a little too high," he said.

They both looked at Elroy to mediate, but he refused, turning around and looking through the bag of papers. Elroy read maps and studied charts to the sound of Patrice and Tobias bickering back and forth. Patrice was arguing that they could save lives by combining both domes, while Tobias wasn't going to bet his life that they had extra food. "What if the shortages are so extreme that they can't spare enough food for our return journey?" Tobias said, "I'm sure they could spare some food for something this important," she said. "What if we get there and the dome is destroyed?" He said. That's impossible!" She said. "If that was the case, then why do we have monthly drills?" He said. "Well, you read the thing; they haven't seen krakens," she said. "But what if, while trying to use the radio in the outpost, they attracted a whole bunch of them," he said. "You know what? Sure, I accept the risk if it means saving people and changing lives for the better," she said. They argued back and forth until Elroy interjected. "How about we sleep on it?" He said, annoyed at all the noise they'd been making. "Fine," they said and climbed onto their bunks. Elroy's ears rang as he tried to sleep.

Chapter 15

Elroy smacked his forehead against the bunk above him. It reminded him of home. Only then did homesickness start to set in. They'd been gone for a month now; he'd be willing to bet that there were missing person signs for all of them. He wished he was back home, where he could stretch his legs and not always be moving. It was only then that he realized that they were moving. Him hitting his head against her bed must've woken Patrice, who also noticed that they were moving. She slid out of her bunk and landed with a thud on the floor. She walked briskly into the cockpit. "Where are we going?" She said with a tone that made it clear that she would start another argument if she didn't get the answer she wanted. "Dome One," he said. "I've already risked my life a few times on this trip; what's one more?" He added with a smile. She left the room, pleased. "Where are we going?" Asked Elroy, rubbing his eyes. "Dome One," she said, sitting down next to him. "Guess he changed his mind," he said. "Yup," she said. After some chitchat, they resigned themselves to yet another game of chess.

Two days later, they all gathered around the forward-facing camera. And the moment they were all waiting for happened. In the distance, they saw the bright lights of another dome. Had they not known, they might have thought it was home. They looked so similar. "That's weird. They must have detected us by now. Why haven't they contacted us yet?" Tobias said. "It attracts krakens, remember," Patrice said. "Yes, but surely the risk is worth it if you saw a submarine from another dome," he said. "First off, they don't know we're from another dome, just that we're an unidentified vessel. Second, they know the risk, and if they don't think it's worth it, then I'm sure as hell not going to risk it," she said. Tobias shrugged. "Fair enough," he said. "So, what are we going to do?" Elroy said. "I don't know, dock, I guess," Tobias said. "Are you crazy?" Patrice said. "Well do you have any better ideas?" Tobias said. When nobody said anything, "I thought not," he said.

They were still a ways away from the dome, at least six hours. Two hours later, a submarine left the dome, and it was huge. It easily dwarfed the Mayflower and, seeing as the Mayflower was unarmed, outgunned them as well. The submarine was on course to catch up to them in an hour. They argued about what to do and eventually came up with a plan, one that Elroy did not like. An hour later, the vessel was within a mile of them, and it deployed its weapons, although it didn't fire them. They could see the primed torpedo tubes from here, among other armaments. And, although she kept this to herself, Patrice was pretty sure that it was nuclear-capable. Once it was clear they were being threatened, Elroy jumped.

He was suited up and had thrown himself out of the moon pool. They were nowhere near the seafloor, though. And he dangled a significant distance from the Mayflower, suspended by his line. He then held out the high-power underwater lamp he had with him. He turned the lamp on and off, aiming it at the submarine. His morse code was pretty bad; he had only learned it in school and hadn't used it since. But he was pretty sure he had 'Friendly' down. He flashed the lights at the submarine a few times. He wasn't surprised when they didn't signal back, as they had no way to communicate back. He was, however, surprised when he wasn't immediately winched back up. Patrice was frantically switching between frequencies on the radio, hoping to find something, but she did not. Tobias was slowly increasing his speed. He wanted to get to the dome as fast as possible without seeming too threatening. He figured the best way to do this would be to increase his speed until the submarine 'escorting' them started getting angry. Patrice was thinking of other frequencies to monitor when she remembered Elroy was dangling from the submarine. She rushed to the room with the moon pool and activated the winch. Eventually, Elroy was back aboard. He quickly took off his helmet. "I'm so sorry!" Patrice said. "Don't worry, I'm fine, and I think it worked," he said, starting to remove his suit. "I've increased our speed! ETA is two hours!" Tobias shouted. Elroy and Patrice spent a tense hour looking at the camera feeds. After that hour, he could see individual buildings. And it looked like the layout of this dome wasn't all that different from theirs. After another half-hour, he could see large crowds gathered near the edge of the dome. They were all sitting in the cockpit when Tobias said, "I think they've opened a bay for us" "I'd hope so; otherwise, we'd be screwed," Elroy said. When they approached the bay, he could see individual people, it looked like some people were standing in ranks, but that was about all he could see. They slowly slid into the pen, and the door closed with an ominous clang behind them. "Okay, this is it,"

Elroy said. "Yeah, so many things could go wrong," Patrice said, worrying. "Knock on wood," Tobias said, rapping his knuckles against the table that the radio sat on. "So, I think it's only fair we pick someone to speak for the group," Elroy suggested; they both pointed at him. "I think it's only fair after dangling you out the back of the submarine," Patrice said. "And that encounter with that tiger eel," Tobias said. "But you saved me from that," Elroy said. Tobias shrugged. "I was never good with words," he said. With that decided, they lined up to the ladder that leads out the currently closed hatch, Elroy in front. He half climbed the ladder and began opening the hatch. It was only then that he realized how bad they all smelled. They were all wearing the same clothes that they'd set off in. And the Mayflower was not built for extended voyages. And as such had few hygiene facilities. All this was realized, though, right as the hatch peeked open and fresh air rushed onto his face.

Chapter 16

The area they emerged into wasn't unlike the old abandoned submarine pens in which the Mayflower started its journey. Though it was much better maintained, with the Mayflower being the dirtiest thing in it, by far. Surrounding the submarine were ranks of soldiers, all with rifles at the ready, though not pointed at them. In front of these soldiers was a man in a red beret, seemingly unarmed. He assumed that he had seen a lot of strange things, but the look on his face when three only technically adults climbed out of the mystery submarine. He had recovered from his shock before Tobias had finished climbing out of the hatch. The man in the red beret walked on top of the Mayflower to meet them halfway. "Greetings, I'm General Weathers," he said with an outstretched hand. "Nice to meet you," Elroy said, accepting the handshake. The man was even stronger than he looked. "Follow me," Weathers said, turning around and walking away, not checking to see if they were following. They did follow, though. And they were led outside of the pens. A block of soldiers surrounded them in every direction as Weathers led them forwards. Elroy looked back, and through his escort, he could see some soldiers attempting to open the hatch on the Mayflower, only to find it was locked tight. As soon as they left the big door that led out of the pens, they were met with a roaring crowd. The soldiers acted as a barrier, keeping out the crowd. Several bright flashes hit him as pictures were taken.

The crowd's emotions were mixed; though most seemed happy, a worrying portion seemed enraged. However, their walk didn't last long as they only walked two blocks before they entered a large, fancy-looking building. They were led up a flight of stairs and into a room. When they opened the door to the room, he figured out that this was a hotel. "This will be your room," Weathers said before leaving with the soldiers. The door closed, and a few seconds of silence passed. "Does anybody else get the feeling that we're not allowed to leave?" Tobias said. They both gave a silent nod. Elroy opened his mouth to speak when there was a knock on the door. Elroy opened the door the find two soldiers holding three plates between them. "A meal," one of the soldiers said, handing the plates to them. One soldier left, and the other closed the door. But he only heard one pair of footsteps leaving; he was pretty sure the other

soldier was standing guard outside their room. When
he looked down at his plate, he realized how hungry
he was, especially for something not canned. A large
chunk of fish was on each plate, and a knife and fork.
They all looked at each other, a silent consideration
that maybe they shouldn't eat it. But this silent
discussion ended when Tobias sat on the bed and ate
with his plate in his lap. Soon, they were all eating.
"Wow," Tobias said once he'd finished his portion.
Tobias laid down on his bed and thoroughly
considered a nap but ultimately decided against it.
They all sat in silence for a few minutes, letting their
stomachs settle. "I call first shower!" Tobias said,
jumping up from his seat on the bed and walking into
the attached bathroom. "Damn, well, I call second!"
Patrice said. After they had all showered, they sat in
the room, enjoying being clean. "Well, we've got two
people to find. My dad and professor Bentley," Elroy
said, breaking the silence. He sat up and walked to the
door. He pulled on the doorknob and was surprised to
find it wasn't locked. As soon as the door swung open,
the soldier outside turned to face and stood at
attention. "Anything you need?" He said. "Um, yes,
I'm looking for an Andrew?" He said. "Sure thing," he
thing, turning and leaving. In about a minute, he

returned with a list of names. "Any of these?" He said, handing the list to Elroy. It was a long list; maybe he should have specified. But he scanned the list once, then again, and a third time, but his dad's name wasn't on the list.

Not long after, there was a knock on the door. Elroy opened the door to see Weathers and a small escort of soldiers. "Follow me," He said sternly. So they did, and he led them down several flights of stairs and through winding corridors. Next, they went down another flight of stairs. Elroy was pretty sure they must be underground. But this level looked nothing like the hotel above them. Instead, it resembled some kind of office, with rows of cubicles and bright, fluorescent lighting. The soldiers stopped as soon as they reached this level and turned and went back up the stairs. Weathers led them into an empty room. The only furnishings were a table lined with uncomfortable-looking chairs.

They were seated at one end of the table, and Weathers sat close to them. Soon, a group of middle-aged men in suits entered the room. They introduced themselves, but their long titles went in one ear and out the other, and Elroy was willing to bet Tobias felt the same. "I bet you're wondering why we brought you here?" The suited man at the head of the table said. "Well, we're here to learn more about your dome!" He said. He gestured toward one of the others, and the barrage of questions started. "What's your industrial capability?" "What's your economic output?" "What is the population?" "How much food do you produce?" "What's your administration like?" "Who's your leader?" "Have you discovered any other domes?" "How many submarines do you have?" "How much fuel do you have left?" "What political ideology would you say you follow?" "What's the age demographic like?" And rather worryingly, "What's your military capability?" They could only answer a few of their questions, and Patrice could give educated guesses for a few more, but most of their questions went unanswered. The group was agitated that they only knew the basics. "Come on! They're basically children; how do you expect them to know all this!" Weathers said, clearly tired of the meeting. While Weathers' remark seemed to calm the group, it did the opposite for the three of them. They were all bristling with comments and assertions that they were as adult as they were. Weathers soon escorted them back to their room, clearly unsatisfied with the answers despite what he had said earlier.

The three of them sat on the floor in a triangle, with the list of names in between them. "He could still be out there," Tobias said. "Or maybe while we were out, he returned?" Patrice offered. "Yeah, I hope so," Elroy said. "Well, who's this professor Bentley guy?" Said Patrice. "Well, a professor, so they probably work at the campus," Elroy said. "How do you know if there's a campus here?" Tobias asked. "I don't know for sure, but the layout seems pretty similar to ours," he said. "Sure, but I don't think we're really allowed to go exploring," Tobias said. "I've got an idea," Elroy said.

"Can I get a list of all your factories and what they produce?" Elroy asked the soldier outside their door. "Why do you need that?" The soldier said. "I want to know how my dome compares to yours," he said. "Yes, right away," the soldier said, walking down the hallway. Elroy looked behind him and saw Patrice and Tobias had changed clothes. Though Elroy hadn't. Tobias was wearing his old jeans that he'd washed. They were very beat up. His shirt was long-sleeved, brown, and nondescript. He also wore a hat, and when he had showered, he had neglected to wash his face, leaving a layer of dirt and grime. He also had his old tool belt around his waist. Patrice was wearing a baggy pair of pants and a long coat that almost reached her knees. She also had a long, deep purple scarf. As soon as the soldier left, Elroy quickly changed into a pair of nondescript jeans and an oversized jacket with a hood big enough to cover most of his facial features. With their impromptu disguises ready, they hurried out the door before the soldier could return. They were surprised that there wasn't more security. A few soldiers were in the lobby, but they managed to sneak by. There was a minor crowd outside the hotel, but they managed to pass by unnoticed. Once they were outside of the view of the hotel, they all released a held breath. "Where to now?" Tobias asked. Elroy spun around, trying to orient himself. It was strange, the general layout was the same, but enough was different that it took him a while to find his way. "Uh, this way, I think," he said. After much paranoid walking, they reached their destination, the campus. It was made up of several large buildings, with a lawn separating them. They walked into the nearest building. It was full of people their age, so they didn't stand out all that much. They suspected that this campus's layout and theirs were similar, but none of them had gone to university or had plans to. "Where are we supposed to go?" Tobias asked. "I don't know. Should we ask someone?" Patrice said. The next time a student passed them, Elroy stopped them. "Hey, do you know where professor Bentley is?" He asked. The student looked like she was their age, but she clearly had somewhere to be. "Yeah, she's currently giving a lecture, so you better hurry, take a left and third door on your right," she said and then hurried off. "You heard her," Elroy said as he began walking, picking up his pace.

When they reached the specified door, Elroy hesitated. He moved to knock on the door but stopped and tried the handle. The door was open. Inside was a lecture hall full of students. And at the front was professor Bentley. She was wearing formal clothes; she had graying hair tied in a braid. She was easily more than twice their age. She was currently talking about... something. It sounded complicated, and he didn't understand any of it. The three of them peeked through the door, seemingly unnoticed. Elroy hesitated; he didn't really want to interrupt. But, as it turns out, Tobias had no such worries and strolled down the room toward the professor. When it was clear that he was walking toward her, she stopped the lecture. "What do you want?" She said, covering the microphone on her collar. "I've got something important to tell you. It's best if you come with me," Tobias said. She would've typically dismissed an interruption like this, but he didn't exactly look like a student. Sure he was the right age, but he looked like he was here to fix something. She stared at him for a few more seconds. "Excuse me," she said into the microphone before taking it off and following Tobias. "What is it?" She said as she followed Tobias down the hallway.

Tobias led her to Patrice and Elroy. "Is there anywhere we could discuss this in private?" He asked, only further intriguing the professor. "Um, we could go to my office, I guess," she said. "Lead the way," Tobias said. When they arrived at her office, she let the three of them in before closing the door. "Okay, what do you want?" She said, sitting down in her chair. "Have you heard about the people from another dome arriving?" He said. "Well, of course, word travels fast," she said. "Well, that's us," Elroy said, setting the stack of papers down on her desk. Her eyes widened. She picked up the now damp stack of papers and briefly leafed through it. "Wow, you're awfully young," she said. Tobias was caught off guard for a moment. "Well, we're adults," he said. "Barely," she said. "Look, It doesn't matter how old we are. We have some questions," Elroy said, cutting off a rant from Tobias.